He wasn't  *for murder.*

And he sure as ~~~~~~~~~~~ed in an espionage ~~~~~~~~~~~ woman he coul~~~~~~~~~

"I want to see that message you intercepted."

She blinked. "You still don't believe me?"

"After everything you've done to me?"

Not bothering to answer, she headed toward the door. But he blocked her path. "I'll only say this once," he said. "I'm in charge here. From here on out, you do what I say."

"I don't take orders from you."

"You do now."

Temper flashed in her eyes. Then she pushed past him and stalked outside the hut.

She'd devastated him before, crushing any illusions he had.

And he'd be damned if she'd make a fool of him twice.

Dear Reader,

We all love to read about soldiers—those courageous, romantic warriors who charge into danger with their guns blazing, risking their lives to slay our enemies and keep us safe. But there are quieter heroes around us, too, people who use their covert skills for the greater good, usually without the fanfare or recognition they deserve. Those are the people I decided to highlight in this new series: the Stealth Knights operating on the periphery of our awareness—semireformed thieves and spies, bad-boy heroes who defeat the evil in our world even as they steal our hearts.

I'm so excited to bring you the first of the Stealth Knights stories, and am especially thrilled to set it in one of my favorite places on earth, the Pyrenees Mountains, a land of lush green valleys, medieval villages and craggy peaks— the perfect setting for heart-stopping romance and high intrigue.

I hope you enjoy the adventure!

Gail Barrett

GAIL BARRETT

High-Risk Reunion

ROMANTIC
SUSPENSE

Recycling programs
for this product may
not exist in your area.

ISBN-13: 978-0-373-27752-0

HIGH-RISK REUNION

Printed in U.S.A.

Books by Gail Barrett

Harlequin Romantic Suspense
Cowboy Under Siege #1672
**High-Risk Reunion* #1682

Silhouette Romantic Suspense
Facing the Fire #1414
Heart of a Thief #1514
To Protect a Princess #1538
His 7-Day Fiancée #1560
The Royal Affair #1601
Meltdown #1610

Silhouette Special Edition
Where He Belongs #1722

*The Crusader
**Stealth Knights

All backlist available in ebook

GAIL BARRETT

always knew she'd be a writer. Who else would spend her childhood grinding sparkling rocks into fairy dust and convincing her friends it was real? Or daydream her way through elementary school, spend high school reading philosophy and playing the bagpipes, and then head off to Spain during college to live the writer's life? After four years she straggled back home—broke, but fluent in Spanish. She became a teacher, earned a master's degree in linguistics, married a coast guard officer and had two sons.

But she never lost the desire to write. Then one day, she discovered a Silhouette Intimate Moments novel in a bookstore—and knew she was destined to write romance. Her books have won numerous awards, including a National Readers' Choice Award and Romance Writers of America's prestigious Golden Heart.

Gail currently lives in western Maryland. Readers can contact her through her website, www.gailbarrett.com.

Dedication:
To my fabulous editor, Susan Litman.
Thank you for believing in me!

Acknowledgments:
I'd like to thank the following people for their help
with this book: Elle Kennedy, Judith Sandbrook,
and Mary Jo Archer for their invaluable critiques;
Kathy Lauten for her information about flash drives;
and Joe Barrett for his expert computer help.
Any mistakes are definitely my own.

Chapter 1

País Vell, the Pyrenees Mountains, 11:37 p.m.

Rafael Navarro dangled from the wall of the medieval castle, the murmur of approaching voices drifting down to him in the inky, moonless night. He went dead still, slid his gaze to the void plunging forty feet below him, and wondered what had gone wrong with his plan. Those guards weren't supposed to arrive yet. He'd spent weeks studying their rotation for the G-6 summit, counting off the intervals of the passing searchlight, calculating the exact time and place to break into the American diplomat's room. And he should have had three more minutes to scale this wall.

Cold sweat beaded his forehead. His back and shoulders throbbed as he clung to the nylon rope. But he schooled himself to absolute stillness, knowing even the slightest shift could move a prong on the grappling hook, drawing the royal guards' attention to him. Behind him, a cool breeze swept down the slopes of the Pyrenees Mountains, the slow, rhythmic clanking of cowbells tightening his nerves.

"You're not seriously going to smoke that." The man's voice came from the wall walk above.

"Why not?" a second man asked. His voice had a belligerent edge. "It's not going to kill anyone."

Except Rafe.

"The hell it won't," the first guard said. "You heard the boss. Anyone who screws up tonight gets fired."

"Yeah, yeah."

Rafe's heart galloped against his rib cage. He'd be dead if he didn't move. *Now.* In a few precious seconds, the searchlight would pass, illuminating him like a dark bug splayed on a silver wall.

But cigarette smoke wisped past. More crucial seconds ticked down. Rafe gritted his teeth, his biceps trembling, every survival instinct screaming at him to go. But he couldn't move, couldn't even change positions to relieve the pressure on his now-numb hands.

"Hombre. Would you come *on?*" the first guard said, echoing Rafe's thoughts. "The next rotation's about to catch up."

"Fine." Disgust tinged the smoker's voice. A glowing cigarette butt streaked over the wall, barely missing Rafe's head. The guards finally pushed away from the ledge, the thud of their receding footsteps fading into the night.

Rafe eased out a breath, but forced himself to wait, counting off several vital heartbeats in case they circled back. Then he powered up the rope in a surge of adrenaline, glad he'd kept up the brutal workouts that enabled him to make this climb even though he'd retired from a life of crime.

Until now.

He reached the medieval battlement and paused again. *Still clear.* His arms aching, the desperate need to hurry flogging his brain, he hoisted himself over the edge. Then he yanked up the rope, pulled the grappling hook from the wall, and ducked—just as the searchlight skimmed overhead.

Too damned close.

His heart pounding, that addictive rush of danger streaming through his veins, he crawled to the ancient watchtower, careful to keep his head under the light's wide range. Then he coiled the rope and tucked it against the wall for his descent. The high-powered beam swept back over the cylindrical tower, past a planked oak door dotted with iron studs.

Now. He leaped up and sprinted to the door. Skidding to a stop, he whipped the lock-pick gun from his back pocket, inserted a tension wrench into the lock and applied the gun. A series of sharp, rapid clicks rent the air.

The lock gave way.

Rafe squeezed through the door, careful not to let the hinges creak, into the darkened alcove that adjoined the diplomat's room. At this height he didn't worry about triggering an alarm. No one got past the armed guards, surveillance cameras and intrusion detection devices on the castle's lower floors—except a third-generation master thief like him.

But he wasn't out of danger yet. He had to find the historic signet ring and get back down that wall—

before the reception ended and the American returned to his room.

Flicking on his penlight, he padded across the antique rug to the Baroque-style bureau. He checked the drawers, peeked behind the huge gilded paintings on the medieval wall. No ring. No hidden safe. He turned toward the bedroom.

A soft, feminine laugh stopped him cold.

His pulse drummed hard. He snapped his gaze to the closed velvet drapes dividing the two rooms. The diplomat had come back early—and he wasn't alone.

Rafe frowned, debating his options, but he didn't have a choice. He had to get that ring tonight. The diplomat was scheduled to present it to País Vell's king in the morning. And if *that* happened, Rafe's bargain with the police chief would be void.

His nerves ratcheting higher, every sense hyperalert, he crept to the floor-length drapes and nudged the edge aside. The cool, musty room was shrouded in darkness—only the faint, golden haze from a bedside lamp penetrated the gloom. Rafe zeroed in on the couple standing across from him on the opposite side of the bed. The woman had her back to him, and the mellow light gilded her naked curves.

No, not naked, he amended, his mouth quirking up in regret. But her back was bare, her gown plunging so low on her hips he could easily imagine the rest.

He allowed his gaze to linger, taking a long, leisurely slide down the sensuous sweep of her spine to the riveting contours of her hips. He couldn't fault the diplomat's taste—or haste. The woman was flawless, at least from the rear. She had sleek, honeyed skin, and centerfold-worthy curves. She wore her dark hair up, exposing the tempting nape of her neck. Loose tendrils danced in the light.

And given the rapt expression on the balding diplomat's face, her front side was better yet.

But Rafe didn't have time to ogle the diplomat's escort. Dragging his attention back to the room, he scanned the wingback chairs hulking in the shadows, the imposing Louis XIV armoire with its carved doors hanging ajar. That ring had to be within reach. But how could he get past the bed to search?

The diplomat tugged off his shirt and tossed it aside, then struggled to pull off a sock. He staggered and lost his balance, lurching against the woman. She steadied them both and laughed.

Rafe stilled, the low, throaty sound jarring something inside him, a memory he'd fought to erase. He whipped his gaze to her smooth velvet skin, the dip of her slender waist, and gave his head a swift shake. It couldn't be her. There was *no damned way*.

Gabrielle Ferrer hadn't set foot in País Vell in years.

"Come on, honey," the diplomat said, enunciating his words too carefully, drawing Rafe's eyes to the wine glasses beside the bed. "You're wearing too many clothes."

He spun her around in a move probably meant to be debonair. Instead he tripped and sprawled back over the bed. The woman fell atop him and laughed again. "Easy there." She pushed herself up to her elbows, bringing her face more fully into the halo of light, and Rafe's heart slammed to a halt. So he hadn't hallucinated that voice. It really was Gabrielle.

Hell of a place to find his ex-fiancée.

He ran his eyes down the elegant swell of her cheekbones, the seductive tilt of her lips. She hadn't changed in the past three years. She still had those hot, sultry eyes, that X-rated mouth.

A body that still fueled his erotic dreams.

The diplomat pawed at her dress, pulling her shoulder strap down her arm, revealing the curves of her ample breasts. Curves Rafe had tasted and teased and touched.

He clenched his jaw. Resentment scorched deep in his gut. She was good, he'd give her that much. The sensual laugh, the come-hither way she tossed her head, baring the tempting skin of her throat. She was every man's fantasy, a siren luring him to erotic bliss.

But she'd only been acting with him.

"Let me get you more wine," she purred to the diplomat, and her husky voice scraped over Rafe's nerves. "Then I'll join you."

She pushed herself off the bed. The neckline of her long gown gaped, exposing a flash of creamy flesh. Her body was perfect, all right—an attribute she used well. She wielded it like a lethal weapon, destroying any man foolish enough to care.

Good thing he was no longer that fool.

Dodging the diplomat's groping hands, she turned to the bedside table, and bent to pour the wine. Rafe watched her in action—wriggling, making her dress tighten over her hips in a move guaranteed to snag the eye. His traitorous blood heating, he clenched his gloved hands into fists, the urge to yank that soft, yielding body against his—and make her *want* him again—riding him hard.

He hissed, furious at his reaction—that even after all this time, he wasn't immune. Each sinuous move knocked his heart off course, sending blood surging straight to his groin.

He shook away the lust with effort, determined to focus on finding that ring. But suspicion swirled inside him, the same uneasy feeling he'd had from the start of this job winging back full force. Why was Gabrielle here? She hardly needed a notch on her belt, and seducing this overweight, middle-aged lothario wasn't her style.

Trying to make sense of her presence, he tracked her suggestive movements with narrowed eyes. It didn't surprise him that she would attend the reception. She moved in rarified social circles as one of the megarich of the world. Not only had she inherited a software conglomerate worth billions, but she'd descended from the landed aristocracy. And as cousin to the prime minister, she had political connections, as well.

All that explained her attendance at the summit's reception. But why this charade with the diplomat? And why return to País Vell *now?*

Unless she was after the same thing Rafe was...

His heart missed a beat. He studied the enticing swell of her hips, the gleam of her naked back, and his brows gathered into a frown. Could she be after the historic ring? But why would she be? She didn't need the money. She didn't collect antiquities. And she'd never shown much interest in the *La Brigada* separatists who claimed the seventeenth-century signet ring—a symbol of their lost homeland—was theirs.

Rafe didn't care about the ring, either. And nothing could have tempted him to risk his precious freedom except one thing—the chance to atone for the past.

But none of that explained Gabrielle.

She glanced over her shoulder, shot the diplomat a heated smile, and Rafe's hold on his temper slipped. Regardless of her motives, he knew one thing. That ring was his. If by some odd twist of fate she *had* come here to steal it, she was out of luck.

She finished pouring the wine, then swiveled toward the bed, holding the glass. Without warning, she glanced up, and her gaze collided with his.

She went stock-still. The color slowly leached from her face. His anger steadily building, Rafe folded his arms and scowled back.

Several seconds dragged past. Gabi stayed rooted in place, gawking at him from across the bed. He deliberately severed the contact, then raked his gaze down the length of her—over her full, ripe breasts and narrow waist, back to her stunning face—and his resentment spiked higher yet. Because if she tried to interfere with his plans...

She gave her head a swift shake, as if to pull herself out of her daze. Then she slipped back into seductress mode, curling her lips into a practiced smile. But her hand trembled, sending wine slopping onto the bed, proving she wasn't as unaffected as she tried to pretend.

Good. She deserved to sweat after the callous way she'd dumped him.

Leaning forward, she handed the diplomat the glass of wine. He gulped it down, then reached out to put it on the bedside table. "Lesh get that dress off," he slurred.

"Right." Her voice came out breathy. She stepped away from the bed. Reaching for the straps on her ball-gown, she sliced her gaze back to Rafe's.

He didn't move. Stark tension arced in the air. He raised a brow in challenge, wondering just how far she'd take this game. Not that he cared. Gabrielle had meant nothing to him for years. And if she wanted to perform an impromptu strip tease, who was he to complain?

Unless this was some sort of trap…

The muscles of his belly tightened, more doubts piling inside. Had she expected him to show up here? Had she been sent here to waylay him? But that made no sense. She couldn't have known his plans. And while she might be an expert seductress, she hadn't faked her surprise.

But then why not sound the alarm? Why not tell the diplomat he was here? What game was she trying to play?

She moistened her lush lower lip with her tongue. The gown's thin straps slithered down. Rafe's gaze dropped to the scraps of fabric clinging precariously to her breasts, just as he knew she'd planned. But if she thought she could manipulate him through his hormones, she was wrong.

She paused, as if to heighten the anticipation.

Damned if it didn't work.

Scowling, he cursed his weakness around this woman. He knew better than to let her suck him in. She'd led him on for years, slumming it with him while she waited for a more *respectable* man to come along.

A sudden snore cut through the air.

Gabrielle abruptly straightened. Rafe spared a glance at the diplomat now passed out cold on the sheets. Still scowling, he jerked apart the drapes and strode across the room, determined to get answers fast. As he neared, Gabrielle's perfume flooded his senses, that unique blend of jasmine and vanilla taunting his nerves.

He stopped and braced his hands on his hips. She

tilted her head back to meet his eyes. "Well, hello, Rafe." Her husky voice rumbled inside him, making him angrier yet.

"Gabrielle." He bared his teeth in a feral smile.

She swayed back, her own smile wavering, the pulse speeding at the base of her throat betraying her unease.

It was about time she started to worry.

Because the real game was about to begin.

Chapter 2

Gabrielle gaped at Rafe in dismay, watching everything she'd worked for crumble apart. Bad enough she'd had to return to País Vell. Worse that she'd had to drug the American diplomat, who'd have one heck of a headache when he finally came to. But now the moment she'd dreaded for three torturous years had arrived—she'd come face to face with Rafael Navarro, the man she'd once desperately loved.

And at the worst possible time. She wasn't prepared. She needed time to erect her defenses. And she couldn't afford to mess up this mission. This was her one opportunity for vengeance, to finally bring down the killer who'd murdered her father, the man she'd worked tirelessly to incriminate for the past three years.

Rafe's gaze skewered hers, making her pulse sprint. She pressed her clammy palms to her thighs, determined not to let him see how thoroughly he disrupted her nerves. It didn't help that he was still outrageously gorgeous with his darkly chiseled face, a sorcerer's black eyes, that thick shock of straight black hair.

Unabashed masculinity radiating from every pore.

He leaned his tall, sinewed body even closer, his furious eyes boring into hers. Stark grooves bracketed his sensual mouth, slashing through the razor stubble covering his jaw, and she battled the urge to step back.

He was still sexy, still potent. *Still dangerous.* And he still had that aura of menace that had always kept her enthralled. He'd called to the wildness latent inside her, luring her to forbidden pleasures, tempting her to shed society's prohibitions, and *live.*

She inhaled, willing away the memories. She couldn't think about the past. And she couldn't worry about Rafe—not with everything she'd worked for at stake. Feigning a poise she didn't feel, she pasted on the knowing, jaded expression she now used to keep men safely at bay.

"Imagine meeting you here," she drawled, injecting a note of bored amusement into her voice. "I thought you'd given up the life of crime."

His black eyes flashed. A muscle twitched in his iron jaw, and another whisper of unease slithered down her spine. Rafe wasn't a man to toy with. He never obeyed the rules, never caved to another's will. And he was impossible to control.

"Once a thief, always a thief, right, Gabrielle?"

Her face burned at the memory. She'd used that excuse to break off their engagement, aiming at his most vulnerable spot. But she couldn't tell him the truth— that she'd had to drive him away. It was the only way she could make sure he survived.

"So why are *you* here?" he countered.

She hitched her shoulder toward the diplomat snoring on the bed. "Isn't it obvious?"

"Yeah." He shot her a scathing look. "But stripping for middle-aged drunks is a new low, even for you."

Hurt razored through her. She struggled not to let Rafe see it, her jaw aching from the effort it took to hold her smile in place. But she couldn't miss the irony—since the last time she'd made love was with him.

"He's not so bad," she gritted out.

"Right. He looks like a real ball of fire in bed."

Her smile frozen, she angled up her chin. "That's none of your business."

"The hell it isn't. You made it my business when you waltzed in on my case."

"Your case?" She managed to scoff. "I've got more right to be here than you do. At least *I* was invited in."

His onyx eyes turned deadly. He shifted closer, his wide shoulders caging her in. She moved back and bumped the nightstand, her heart tripping through her chest.

"Cut the crap, Gabrielle. Why are you really here?"

She tried again to inch backward. Her breath dammed up in her lungs. Rafe was too big, too close. *Too threatening.* Warnings skittered inside her, igniting the urgent need to flee.

But he didn't budge. He towered over her, his broad chest filling her vision, sharp intelligence blazing in his eyes.

She frantically shuffled through options, desperate to make him back off. She couldn't tell him the truth, but he'd see through any lies. Maybe the partial truth would satisfy his curiosity, enough to persuade him to leave.

"Fine. If you must know, I'm looking for information."

"What kind of information?"

"Business. Something that affects FerrCom, my corporation. It has nothing to do with you."

At least not directly. She'd recently intercepted a message using her company's secret backdoor access to the billing software they ran. The message revealed that the American diplomat would deliver some highly sensitive intelligence to the king at the G-6 summit, exposing the identity of a traitor in the king's inner circle.

The trouble was, the police chief—the man she believed to be the traitor—had access to the communications, too. And she knew he would never allow that intelligence to reach the king. She had to confiscate it before he did and deliver it to the prime minister, head of an ultrasecret spy group dedicated to protecting the king.

Resolve settled inside her. She'd waited three long years for this opportunity to destroy the police chief— the man who'd murdered her beloved father and assaulted her.

And this time she wouldn't fail.

"You're stealing from your competitors?" Rafe's voice rang with outrage, drawing her attention back to him. "After claiming *my* criminal background would hurt your career?"

She tried not to wince. She'd only said that to drive him away. "I might as well. I learned to steal from the best."

His eyes turned glacial. And guilt caught her square

in the gut. She didn't want to hurt him. She'd already caused him enough pain.

And she _knew_ he'd gone straight—at least, until now. Shortly after they'd met he'd severed his ties to his tight-knit family, making himself an outcast, sacrificing everything he cared about to uphold the law.

But she had to throw him off her trail. She couldn't risk that he'd discover the truth about the past—or get too close to her now.

"So why are _you_ really here?" she asked again.

"I'm looking for jewelry."

"In the castle? During the summit?" Even an adrenaline junkie like Rafe wouldn't have the gall.

"You know me—always aiming out of my league."

She flinched, the haughty words she'd used to reject him flaying _her_ now. But she bit down hard on her lip to keep from blurting out a defense. It was safer for them both if he believed the worst.

No matter how badly his derision stung.

She studied his furious eyes, still unable to believe he'd resumed a life of crime. But what else could he be up to? He couldn't possibly know about the intelligence she sought.

She shook her head. She'd have to puzzle that out later. She needed to get what she came for and leave—before the diplomat came to.

"Great," she said, trying to sound offhand. "Then we won't be in each other's way. You can hunt for jewelry, and I'll look for that information I need."

Her composure rattled, she swiveled back to the bed. Trying hard to ignore Rafe still looming beside her, she got to work—punching the pillows and tangling the sheets, tugging off the diplomat's pants. She couldn't hide her presence in the diplomat's bedroom. Dozens of guests had seen them leave the reception together, and the surveillance cameras had recorded them walking through the halls to his room. Her only chance to avoid suspicion when he discovered the missing intelligence was to give the appearance that they'd had sex.

She grabbed the diplomat's glass from the nightstand and turned toward the bathroom—but Rafe still barred her way. He stood with his feet planted wide, his muscled arms folded over his chest, his cynical eyes tracking her moves.

Her stomach churning, she pushed past him. She didn't care what he thought. She'd come here for justice, not forgiveness—especially from him.

She marched into the adjacent bathroom, her high heels clicking on the medieval stones, then glanced in the bathroom mirror. Behind her, Rafe finally began prowling around the bedroom, and she let out a pent-up breath. Lord, she didn't need this. Returning to País Vell was dangerous enough. Hopefully he'd give up on finding valuables and leave before this night got worse.

Still keenly aware of Rafe's movements, she rinsed out the diplomat's wine glass, erasing traces of the drug she'd used, then returned it to the nightstand by the bed. To be safe, she swirled in some untainted wine.

Hesitating, she studied the nearly nude diplomat, his gray-haired chest rising with every ragged snore. Deciding to add another touch, she ripped a page from the notepad by the telephone, jotted down that she'd enjoyed the night, and left it on the pillow beside his head.

That done, she set to work. Following in Rafe's footsteps, she searched the room—rifling through the drawer in the bedside table, checking the diplomat's suitcase, examining the pockets and seams of his clothes. She assumed he'd put the information she needed on a computer flash drive or something equally as easy to transport.

But where had he squirreled it away?

She rummaged through the antique armoire as Rafe looked under the bed. *Still nothing.* Frustrated, she re-entered the bathroom and checked his toiletry case.

A soft *click* from the bedroom reached her ears. Whirling back, she spotted Rafe kneeling beside a brief-case on the floor. Her pulse quickening, she rushed to his side. "Let me see that," she said.

He didn't answer. Instead, he opened the briefcase and thumbed through the folders, then pulled out a small velvet bag. He loosened the drawstring and dumped the contents into his palm. A large gold ring gleamed against his black leather glove.

Her jaw dropped. So he really had come here in search of jewels. But why? He'd quit his family's busi-ness years ago.

Still holding the ring, he rose, slipped it back into the velvet bag, then stuffed it into the pocket of his jeans.

She stared at him in disbelief. "You're not really going to take that."

"Damn straight I am."

"But…you can't. I'll get blamed." Too much evidence placed her in the room. And stealing the flash drive was one thing. She needed that to bring down a murderous traitor, an end she could justify. But a ring… "You have to put it back."

"Forget it." He turned toward the long, velvet drapes.

Panic swarmed inside her. "Rafe, please," she begged. "This is going to mess everything up."

His head swung around. The fury in his eyes stopped her cold. "I'm a *thief,* Gabrielle. This is what I do. So why should I put it back?"

She clenched her hands, her stomach in total turmoil as he flung her words back at her. But she couldn't explain why she'd lied, why she'd had to push him away. She could *never* let him know.

But if she got arrested for the theft… The police chief would get away with her father's murder. He'd lock her behind bars—or worse.

"Listen," she pleaded. "I know I'm asking a lot, but you have to believe me—"

"Believe you?" He let out a bitter laugh. "After the way you lied to me?"

"I didn't—"

A man's voice rose in the hallway, cutting her off. She froze in sudden alarm. Someone was coming. Oh, God. *She had to go.*

But she hadn't found the flash drive yet.

"Expecting someone?" Rafe asked.

"What? No, of course not." How could he think that?

Footsteps thudded outside the door. Her entire body tensed.

"Secure the stairs," the man called out. "I'll check the bedroom."

Her stomach plunged. *Raymundo Ortiz.* The police chief. The man who'd slaughtered her father and nearly murdered her.

She stared at the door in horror, knowing she had to flee. But if she ran, she'd look guilty. And she hadn't done anything wrong—aside from slipping the diplomat that drug. But did she dare stay and try to brazen it out, and confront that cold-blooded killer alone?

Rafe shot her a glare, as if *she'd* conjured up Ortiz, then pushed through the velvet drapes. The doorknob rattled hard. Her pulse went berserk. No way was she taking on Ortiz. She turned and rushed after Rafe.

She caught up with him at the alcove door. He whipped around, anger rolling off him in waves. "What do you want now?"

"I'm leaving."

"Not with me, you aren't."

"Then move aside." Frantic, she tried to step around him. He shot out his arm and blocked her way. "Are you crazy? You can't just go waltzing out there. The guards will shoot you on sight."

"I can't stay in here."

"The hell you can't."

"Rafe, please." More thumps rose from the bedroom door, and her desperation surged. "Let me by. I can't let him find me. *I have to go.*"

He scowled at her for several heartbeats, then hissed. "Fine, follow me. But you have to do what I say. I mean it." His fierce gaze burned into hers. "You make one wrong move and you're on your own." Motioning for her to be quiet, he cracked open the alcove door.

Relieved he'd agreed to help her, she shot a nervous glance at the drapes. Ortiz must have come for the flash drive. He must have seen her leave the reception with the diplomat and somehow divined her plans. But why bring backup? Why advertise his presence? Shouldn't he sneak into the bedroom alone?

Rafe glanced her way. "Stay close."

He didn't have to warn her. Ortiz ran the royal police. His armed guards swarmed the castle. It would take a miracle to escape.

Rafe crept onto the medieval wall walk. She scurried after, trying not to make any noise. Dressed all in black, he instantly merged with the shadows. Her heart beat triple time as she dogged his heels.

He strode to the nearby watch tower and picked up a bundle of rope—which came as no surprise. Rafe had always prepared his heists meticulously, calculating every contingency—his secret to avoiding arrest.

But suddenly, he wheeled around, grabbed her arm, and shoved her against the tower. She gasped. "What—?"

"Shh!"

He flattened his body against hers. The rough rocks dug at her bare back. A second later, a guard charged by, his rifle raised, his heavy boots pounding the stones.

And a wild sound wedged in her throat. She hadn't even heard him coming. If it hadn't been for Rafe, she'd be dead.

The guard reached the alcove door. He kicked it open and charged inside.

"Come on." Rafe seized her arm, but he didn't have to convince her to rush. She raced across the uneven wall walk beside him, running as fast as she could in her wobbly heels.

They flew past another watch tower, then jumped down a flight of stone steps. Shouts rose from the courtyard below them, and she prayed the crenellated edge of the battlement would keep them concealed.

But a minute later, Rafe stopped again. "Get down!"

She dove to the ground, heedless of the sharp stones scraping her legs through her flimsy dress, and pressed her back to the wall. A heartbeat later, the searchlight skipped overhead.

She struggled to breathe. A siren rose in the distance, adding more confusion to her already disordered thoughts. Why the show of force? She hadn't done anything wrong as far as the police chief knew.

Unless he was chasing Rafe…

But that didn't make sense. Rafe had planned this job down to the second, even timing the searchlight. How had Ortiz known that he'd broken in?

Rafe leaned close. His warm breath feathered her ear. "We'll climb down here. I'll go first. As soon as I'm clear, grab the rope and slide down."

"Slide?" Down a three-story wall?

"There's no time to lower you down." He pulled off his leather gloves and pressed them into her hands. "Wear these. And move fast. We've only got three minutes to beat the light."

"Right." Fighting back a burst of anxiety, she slipped on the supple gloves, still warm from his big hands. Then she tugged off her strappy sandals and looped them over her wrists. She could do this. She *had* to do this. It was the only way to survive.

The powerful beam passed by. Rafe jumped to his feet, secured the grappling hook to the wall, and tossed the rope over the side. Gabi scrambled upright as he climbed onto the ledge.

She glanced down, but the obsidian night swallowed the ground. She quickly averted her gaze, trying not to think about the deadly drop—or what would happen if she fell.

Rafe pushed off, twirled around and planted his feet on the wall. Then his dark gaze connected with hers, and for an instant, time seemed to grind to a halt. And that old sense of adventure zipped back, that heady feeling of excitement he'd always evoked. Rafe had jolted her from her sheltered upbringing, giving her a thrilling taste of danger she couldn't resist. He'd been off-limits, forbidden. A thief. A man society didn't approve of. A man who'd made her feel intensely alive.

"Hurry," he urged, then disappeared into the dark.

Bunching up the hem of her ball gown, she swung her legs over the ledge. Another siren joined the first one. Footsteps thundered close by. Knowing she only had seconds, she leaned down and grabbed the rope, her stomach a riot of nerves. Then she sucked in a breath and leaped.

For a second, she couldn't move. She clutched the rope with a death grip, too terrified to loosen her hold. Her shoulders began to ache. The night wind chilled her bare back. The rope undulated wildly beneath her as Rafe worked his way to the ground, and it was all she could do to hang on.

But she had to move. She had to get away from the wall walk before the guards caught up—or her arms gave way and she fell.

Summoning her courage, she pried her fingers apart. She instantly flew downward, the rope tearing through her hands. *Too fast.*

Startled, she tightened her grip and jolted to a stop, badly wrenching her arms. She panted wildly, so scared she could hardly think.

But the footsteps were pounding closer. She didn't have time to waste. Slackening her grip, she inched down the nylon rope, sliding and stopping in erratic bursts. Her momentum spun her around, banged her against the wall, and she tried not to let out a moan.

Endless seconds crawled past. Her palms burned despite the leather gloves. Her arms trembled violently, her shoulder muscles searing as she struggled to hold on to the rope. She had no idea how much time she had left—or how many yards to the ground.

Suddenly an arm encircled her waist. Panicked, she gasped and clutched the rope. But Rafe's voice murmured into her ear. "Let go. You made it." Shaking, her legs wobbling so hard she couldn't stand, she collapsed on the hard-packed dirt.

"Run," he urged her. "Get into the woods."

Still panting, she lifted her head. She caught the flash of the oncoming searchlight—and a fresh surge of adrenaline zapped her into gear. She lurched to her feet, gathered her hem so she wouldn't trip, then ran full-out toward the woods.

But she realized Rafe wasn't with her. She whirled around, spotted him still standing by the wall, whipping the long rope back and forth. A moment later, the grappling hook thudded into the ground.

He scooped up the rope, tossed it into a nearby bush, and began sprinting her way. She spun back into motion, Rafe's footsteps spurring her on. The searchlight swung steadily closer. She desperately tried to speed up. They only had seconds to reach the trees.

Rafe flew past her and grabbed her arm. She plunged with him into the undergrowth—but then lost her balance and fell. Branches tore at her face, her hair, her arms. She crashed to the ground, her skin stinging, her breath knocked from her lungs. A fraction of a second later, the searchlight passed overhead.

Shaking wildly, her heart stampeding out of control, she lay sprawled in the prickly brush. She waited, not daring to move, as the beam swung past her again.

"This way," Rafe called softly.

Still breathless, she slipped on her flimsy sandals to protect her feet. Then she rose and battled her way through the bushes, the sharp branches snagging her dress. She jerked it loose, ignoring the sound of ripping fabric as she stumbled through the woods after Rafe.

A wild feeling burbled inside her at the disaster she'd made of the night. She hadn't found the flash drive. The police chief might now have it—destroying her only proof of his crimes. And she was fleeing the castle with Rafe—the one man she'd vowed to avoid.

So what should she do? She tripped on an exposed tree root, struggling to remain upright in the steep terrain. She couldn't stay with Rafe, she knew that much. He was a wild card in this fiasco, uncontrollable. She couldn't take the chance that he would expose her—or discover the truth about the past.

But Ortiz had seen her at the reception. He now knew she'd returned to País Vell. And if he guessed that she knew about his secret activities, he'd stop at nothing to hunt her down.

Rafe came to a halt. "Hold up."

She bumped against him, then craned her neck to see. "What is it?"

"We've reached the road."

She peered through the thick foliage. A blue LED light flashed below them, illuminating the two-lane road that switchbacked down the mountain into the town. *"The police."*

"It looks like they've set up a roadblock." Rafe's low voice rumbled through the dark. "Stay here. I'll see what I can find out."

Without waiting for an answer, he crept off. Car doors slammed nearby. A radio squawked from the road. Gabi shivered and rubbed her arms, the night chill settling into her bones.

And the horror of her predicament spun through her mind. She'd bungled her mission badly. She'd somehow tipped off Ortiz, a man with unlimited power. But she couldn't give up. She had to find that proof. No matter what else happened, she had to destroy her father's murderer. This was her only chance.

A twig snapped close by. She spun around, alarmed, as a shadow materialized at her side. "It's me," Rafe murmured, and she pressed her palm to her rioting heart.

"What's going on?" she whispered, her eyes searching his in the dark.

"They're looking for us, all right."

"Both of us?" She frowned. "Did you hear why?"

"Yeah." He paused. His eyes turned even more grim. "They think we've committed a murder."

"Murder?" she gasped.

He nodded, his mouth hardening into a slit. "The diplomat is dead."

Chapter 3

"I didn't kill him." Gabi trailed Rafe through the woods in the darkness, still struggling to wrap her mind around the diplomat's death. "That drug I gave him…it only made him drowsy. It couldn't have caused a reaction. And I know he didn't have allergies because I had his medical records checked."

Rafe didn't answer. He continued to push through the bushes, using his tiny penlight to illuminate the rocky ground.

"I mean it, Rafe." She slid on a pinecone, nearly falling in her awkward designer heels. "There's no way that drug could have killed him."

"I believe you." He stopped, then waited for her to catch up. "The police said he was shot."

"Shot?" She stumbled to a halt. "But who… *Ortiz?*"

Rafe's mouth tightened, his face barely visible in the night. "Who else?"

Her heart took a nosedive. This was so much worse than she'd thought. But why would Ortiz kill the diplomat? Why not simply steal the flash drive while he slept? None of this made sense.

Then even more horror dawned, and she pressed her hand to her throat. "They've got evidence against me. I left the reception with him. I'm on the security tapes. *I left that note.*"

Then another realization slammed into the first one, making her head spin even more. "Oh, God. It *was* my fault. I drugged him. He couldn't even defend himself. I left him there to die."

She hugged her arms, guilt crashing through her, a terrible tightness welling up in her throat. "I didn't mean to hurt him." All she'd wanted was justice for her father's death. Instead, she'd condemned an innocent man to die.

Stricken, she shook her head. "I shouldn't have left. I should have stayed there and protected him."

"Then Ortiz would have killed you, too."

But why? What did Ortiz have to gain from their deaths, aside from silencing *her?*

"What a mess," she whispered, dazed. The evening had turned into a nightmare, and it just kept getting worse. She'd taken a chance by returning to País Vell. Certain she would find that flash drive, she'd planned to confiscate the evidence and turn it over to the prime minister before Ortiz could do her harm. But everything had gone wrong. And now she would never escape Ortiz. He had too much power—aircraft and weapons at his disposal, a police force at his command. He would launch a massive manhunt and scour the surrounding hills.

And then, yet another bolt of awareness struck home. She didn't only need to elude Ortiz. The Americans would hunt for her, too. They would search the globe to find their diplomat's supposed killer—leaving her no safe place to hide.

Panic rising inside her, she shot a furtive glance around the inky woods. She couldn't waste time. She had to stay on the move, get farther away from the castle before Ortiz and his men caught up—and then figure out what to do.

"Come on. We need to keep moving," Rafe said, echoing her thoughts. "There's an old shepherd's hut near here. We can rest there for a while and make plans."

"You think it's safe?"

"For tonight. I scouted it out earlier. It's been abandoned for decades, probably since the Spanish civil war. The vegetation is overgrown, and there's nothing else nearby. I doubt anyone remembers it's there."

He resumed hiking. She followed more slowly, her reservations growing as she picked her way through the brush—but she didn't have much choice. She needed to stick with Rafe until she formed an alternate plan.

But Rafe presented dangers of his own. He was too clever, too suspicious. He knew her far too well, making it hard to hide the truth.

Which meant before he figured out what she was up to, she had to get away from *him*.

Several exhausting miles later, they reached the abandoned hut. Gabi huddled on a stool by the rustic fireplace, watching Rafe feed scraps of kindling into the sparks. The tiny flames licked the wood, casting firelight over his arms. The scent of wood smoke snaked through the air.

She shivered and rubbed her feet, her open sandals no protection against the bone-shuddering chill seeping through the dirt floor. Adding to her misery, the night breeze gusted through holes in the old tile roof, raising goose bumps along her skin.

Rafe leaned back on his heels and cut her a brooding look. Suddenly he peeled off his black turtleneck sweater, leaving on a short-sleeved T-shirt, and tossed the sweater to her. "Put that on before you freeze to death," he said.

Too cold to argue, she tugged it over her head. The soft cotton sweater smelled faintly of Rafe's aftershave, a sandalwood blend she'd always loved. She hugged her arms, the familiar scent giving her comfort, grateful for the added warmth.

For a minute they didn't speak. Rafe stared at the fire, his rough-hewn, masculine profile illuminated by the flickering light. She scanned the width of his bulging shoulders, the curve of his iron biceps, the sinews in his strong neck.

Then his eyes returned to hers, the impact changing the rhythm of her pulse. "All right. Let's hear it."

"Hear what?"

His mouth flattened in a sign of impatience. "What you were really doing back there."

"But I already told you—"

"Cut the lies, Gabrielle."

The bitterness in his voice brought her up short. "You don't believe me?"

"Of course I don't believe you."

"But…I'm telling you the truth."

"The truth?" He barked out a cynical laugh. "You never told me the truth in your life."

Her stomach churned. She looked away, knowing she deserved his scorn. She'd treated him abominably that night. She'd hurled cruel, hurtful lies at him, willingly crushing his heart. But she'd done it to protect him. *She'd had to drive him away.*

But she couldn't tell him that. She had to keep that secret buried, no matter what the cost.

Inhaling deeply to steady herself, she leveled her voice. "I told you. I came here for information—for my business. It doesn't affect you at all."

"Right. And we both just happened to be there when Ortiz showed up."

His words stopped her cold. Startled, she searched his eyes. "You're saying you weren't there by chance?"

He made a sound of disgust. "Come on, Gabrielle. You know damned well that Ortiz set me up."

She stared at him in shock. "You think he set *you* up? How?"

"As if you don't know."

"I don't."

He bunched his jaw, the planes of his dark face hard. The fire crackled in the now-tense air.

"I really don't, Rafe. What does he have to do with you?"

His jaw still working, he turned his gaze to the fire. After a minute, he sighed. "He hired me to steal that ring."

"He *hired* you?" She gaped at him, staggered, certain that she'd heard wrong. Rafe was working for Ortiz, the man who'd murdered her father?

Could this night get any more bizarre?

"But…you hate Ortiz." He'd persecuted Rafe's family for decades, scapegoating them for a myriad of crimes. The thought of Rafe now collaborating with his arch-enemy defied logic—and boggled her mind. "Why on earth would you work for him?"

He didn't answer at first. He kept his gaze on the flames. Then the cool wind gusted, scattering sparks over the dirt, and he slanted her a glance. "He came to my shop last week," he said, referring to the precious gem business he ran. "He stops by once in a while and accuses me of fencing jewels." He grimaced. "He doesn't think I've reformed, either."

Her cheeks burned. She bit back the denial that instantly sprang to her lips. She had to let him think the worst. "And?"

"He offered me a job."

"To steal that ring." She couldn't keep the incredulity from her voice.

Rafe tilted his head. "He said the diplomat would be bringing it to the summit as a goodwill gesture to the king. The Americans want his cooperation in their war on terror."

That made sense. País Vell had a long history of smuggling given its strategic location between Spain and France. Information—and criminals—often slipped through the porous hills.

"But the ring belonged to the last queen of Reino Antiguo," Rafe continued, naming the once-independent kingdom now controlled by País Vell. "Ortiz knew the separatists would protest if they found out the king had it. So he hired me to find it. He wanted to keep it hidden until the summit ended so there wouldn't be any unrest."

That seemed plausible, too. The last thing the police

would want during an important international summit was rioting in the streets. "But wouldn't that cause problems with the Americans? They'd hardly overlook the theft."

Rafe shrugged. "He seemed more concerned about the separatists. And he planned to give the ring back after the summit...or so he said. He probably figured he could placate the Americans for a few days."

She frowned at that. The story sounded logical—up to a point. "But why hire you? Why not get it himself?"

"He said there were separatist sympathizers on the police force so he couldn't send in his own men."

"But then why show up at the room?"

"Exactly." He dipped his head. "He obviously set me up."

The breeze gusted again, raising more goose bumps on her spine as she turned that over in her mind. Ortiz was clever, ruthless. She could see him concocting this plan. He could arrest Rafe at last, claiming he'd caught him stealing the ring. He could even blame him for the diplomat's murder. No one would believe Rafe's word over his.

But why would Rafe take such an obvious risk?

"What did you get out of this?" she asked.

"Nothing."

"But—"

"Forget it. It's personal. It has nothing to do with you. What matters is that he set me up."

His brusque tone hurt, but she could hardly fault him for shutting her out. Rafe was a fiercely loyal man. He would never forgive a betrayal.

Especially hers.

Her throat suddenly thick, she returned her gaze to

the fire. And she had to admit that Rafe had changed in the past three years. The tender man who'd teased her, the thrilling daredevil who'd fulfilled her need for adventure had disappeared. He was harder now, more cynical. He had a deep-seated bitterness to him—hostility and resentment she'd caused.

A dull ache hollowed her chest, kicking off a swarm of regrets. She'd never wanted to hurt him. She'd adored Rafe. She would have given anything to spend her life in his arms.

But she'd made the right choice. She'd *had* to break off their engagement. If she'd told him the truth, he would have gone after Ortiz. And there was no earthly way she could have risked Rafe's life.

Taking a deep steadying breath, she struggled to corral her unruly emotions and think. She couldn't change the past. She couldn't erase her lies—or the terrible pain she'd caused. She couldn't even tell Rafe the truth. All she could do was focus on her mission and find the proof she needed to destroy Ortiz—before more innocent people died.

Rafe was right, though. Ortiz did nothing by chance. And she couldn't believe that he'd coincidentally hired Rafe to get that ring at the same time that intelligence was coming in. That ring *had* to be connected to her case.

But how?

"May I see the ring?" she asked, rising.

Rafe hesitated—which stung. "I'm not going to run off with it," she said, her voice tight.

"You've got that right." He pulled the velvet bag from his pocket and tossed it her way.

She caught it, then moved closer to the fire, determined to ignore the lash of hurt. No matter how much his distrust galled her, no matter how strong the urge to explain and beg his forgiveness, she had to focus on what mattered now.

She loosened the bag's tassled drawstring, then dumped the heavy ring into her palm. Made of solid gold, it had a flat, square top with the relief of a bearded vulture—the bone crusher, Reino Antiguo's royal crest. The gold simmered like fire in the light.

"It's beautiful." She tilted it toward the flames, studying the words engraved on the thick band. "There's an inscription…in Latin. *Morior invictus.* Death before defeat."

Rafe nodded. "Reino Antiguo's motto. The ring was used as a royal seal."

Not a secret message, then—unless the ring was fake. She caught Rafe's eye. "You think it's real?"

"It looks authentic. I'd have to examine it to be sure, though." His gaze sharpened. "Why? You think there's a connection to the information you're looking for?"

Of course Rafe would figure that out. Keeping her expression neutral, she slipped the ring back into the bag. "I don't see how."

But if there *was* a connection to her case, she needed to keep the ring. She'd spent too many years waiting for this moment to lose any evidence now.

But Rafe would never give it up. He'd stolen it for Ortiz, which put them squarely at odds.

She handed Rafe the velvet pouch. He shoved it into his front pocket, his perceptive gaze trained on her. And she knew he was sorting through details, deciding whether to believe her or not.

"So what's your plan?" she asked, hoping to distract him.

"We'll rest for now. We can start hiking again at dawn. The terrain's too rough from here on out. I don't want to fall off a cliff."

That bought her a couple hours. But it meant staying in the hut with him.

She glanced around the miniscule room—the rickety bed, the two wooden stools by the fireplace, the peeling stucco walls. And suddenly, she needed air, space. "I'll be right back."

"You still owe me answers," he warned as she headed for the door. "Don't even think of running away."

So he'd decided not to trust her.

Smart man.

"I said I'd be back." And she would. She couldn't run yet, not without that ring. And she couldn't get *that* until Rafe slept.

She opened the door and stepped outside, then slumped back against the hut's stone wall. She inhaled deeply, filling her lungs with the crisp night air, and tried to calm herself down. Cowbells clanked in the distance, the discordant sound doing nothing to assuage her nerves.

The diplomat was dead. She still didn't have that flash drive. And now Rafe had a ring that might be connected to her case—which meant she had to steal it from him.

A fresh wave of anxiety tumbled through her, her conscience rebelling at the thought of deceiving Rafe *again*. He'd be furious when she took that ring. She would confirm every terrible suspicion about her he had.

She closed her eyes, fighting back an onslaught of

regrets. She didn't want to hurt him. She hated that he despised her, and that she couldn't reveal the truth. But Ortiz had robbed her of choices that fateful night.

And nothing mattered more than revenge.

The soft swish of Gabrielle's dress woke Rafe from a restless doze. He lay flat on his back by the fireplace, keeping his eyes shut, his breathing steady and slow to imitate sleep.

So she was finally making her move. He'd been expecting it for hours. He hadn't missed the speculation in her eyes when she'd held that ring or the way she'd sidestepped his questions, never quite revealing why she was here.

He intended to get those answers now.

Her footsteps shuffled closer. He waited, his pulse accelerating as the erotic scent of her perfume mingled with smoke from the dying fire.

The swishing stopped. He felt her studying his face. Then she knelt beside him, her silk gown brushing his arm, her soft breath sweeping his jaw as she slid her fingers into the front left pocket of his jeans.

He gritted his teeth, struggling to regulate his breath as her fingers inched down his thigh. But his temper flared, his blood roiling at her gall. She'd accused *him* of being a thief—while here she was, trying to steal the ring from him.

Her hand came to a halt. For a minute, she didn't move. Then she caught the velvet pouch between her fingers and started to tug.

He whipped out his hand and clamped her wrist. Her startled gaze flew to his. For several long seconds their eyes stayed locked, her pulse running ragged beneath his palm.

Then he relentlessly tugged her closer, until her face was inches from his. "Looking for something?" he growled.

Her gaze faltered. She nibbled her bottom lip, drawing his eyes to her sultry mouth. Then she relaxed against him, morphing into seductress mode, and shot him a sideways glance. "Can't you guess?" she purred.

He took in her full pouting lips, the swell of her generous breasts, and his hold on his temper slipped. She was playing him, trying to manipulate him with her charms—just like she'd done to that diplomat.

His mouth thinned. "Nice performance. What's next? Another striptease?"

Her eyes flashed. She struggled to jerk her hand free, but he squeezed her wrist even harder, unwilling to let her budge. He waited for several heartbeats, making sure she knew she couldn't escape him, then pushed her away in disgust.

He rolled to his feet, then stalked to the door and back, trying to keep himself under control. When he reached the fireplace, he stopped. "All right," he said. "Cut the crap and start talking—beginning with why you're really here."

She rose and brushed off her gown, her eyes not quite meeting his. "I already told you. I'm after information."

"The hell you are."

"I am," she insisted. He waited, barely managing to restrain his temper, until her guilty gaze rose to his. "It's just…I think the ring might be involved."

"How?"

"I don't know." He shot her a scowl, and she lifted her chin. "I don't. It's…complicated."

"Try me."

She hesitated.

His jaw hardened. "That wasn't a request."

Her movements jerky, she retreated to the stool beside the fireplace and sat. The wind gusted, moaning through the caved-in roof, making the embers in the fireplace flare.

"I told you the truth," she said finally, her voice subdued. "At least most of it. You know my company makes billing software for communication firms."

He nodded, and she went on. "Whenever we install a system we keep a secret backdoor access in case we need to do repairs. And…we use that to monitor their calls."

She spied on them? And she'd accused *him* of immoral behavior? "That's illegal."

She had the grace to blush. "I know. And our customers don't know we do that, obviously. If people knew we kept track of their activities, they wouldn't buy our products."

Which they marketed to governments around the globe.

He leaned against the mantle, wondering where she was heading with this. "Go on."

"I didn't know about the backdoor access at first. It's hardly something we advertise. But after my father died, when I took over the company, I started noticing irregularities. I finally figured out he was checking messages that way. And I think he found out something incriminating, something dangerous that got him killed."

Rafe blinked, her revelation taking him aback. Whatever he'd expected her to say, it wasn't that.

He swung his gaze to the glowing embers, searching his memory for details of the case. Her father had died at his office during a late-night robbery. His murder—and Gabi's subsequent ascent to owner of the company—had prompted her to break off her engagement to Rafe.

"You're saying he wasn't robbed?"

"That's right. The murderer just made it look that way." Her gaze swerved back to his. "My father was spying for the government, running a secret operation Arturo Menendez—the prime minister—heads. We think he came across some information in one of those messages, something that someone didn't want to leak out."

"Did you tell the police?"

"No." She smoothed her long gown over her legs. "I couldn't prove anything at the time. And except for the prime minister, I didn't know who to trust. He suggested we get proof before we accuse anyone."

Too bad the police didn't do the same.

Rafe pushed his resentment aside. "So where does the diplomat fit in?"

"A few weeks ago I intercepted a message. He was supposed to deliver some top-secret intelligence at the summit about a traitor in the king's inner group.

"I figured the information would be on a flash drive," she added. "That's what I was looking for in the room. I didn't know about the ring. And the ring might just be a coincidence—a goodwill gesture like the police chief said. But if there's any chance it's connected to my father's murder, I have to find out. I can't let his killer go free."

Rafe's frown deepened, her revelation complicating an already unholy mess. If Ortiz wanted that ring, and if that ring was connected to her case…

His gaze sharpened on hers. "You're saying Ortiz is the traitor?"

"I don't know."

"But you think he is."

"I don't have any proof."

Hell. Suddenly feeling haunted, Rafe plowed his hand through his hair. This job was supposed to be straightforward—grab the ring, turn it over to the police chief and fulfill his end of the deal.

He wasn't supposed to be framed for murder. He wasn't supposed to be chased by the royal guards. And he sure as hell wasn't supposed to be embroiled in an espionage case involving his former lover—a woman he couldn't trust.

He eyed Gabi's thick, tousled hair, the tempting bow of her lips and everything inside him rebelled. He didn't need her hanging around him. He wanted to forget he'd ever seen her and get her permanently out of his life.

But he couldn't escape the facts. Ortiz had framed him for the diplomat's murder. This case was far more complicated than he'd believed. And like it or not, whatever Gabi was searching for impacted him—which meant he had to keep her around.

But he also had to be careful. He had too much at stake to let down his guard around her now. "I want to see that message you intercepted."

She blinked. "You still don't believe me?"

"After everything you've done to me?"

Her amber eyes turned wounded, but he crushed down an answering spurt of guilt. She was acting again, trying to play on his sympathies, and he refused to take the bait.

He glanced at his watch. "It's nearly dawn. We can head out now."

Not bothering to answer, she rose and headed toward the door. But he quickly stepped around her and blocked her path. "I'll only say this once," he said when she lifted her gaze to his. "I'm in charge here. From here on out, you do what I say."

Her eyes filled with outrage, just as he'd known they would. "I don't take orders from you."

"You do now. I'm warning you, Gabi. You try to sneak off, you try to stab me in the back or steal that ring, and you'll be sorry you tried."

Her mouth tightened. Annoyance flashed in her golden eyes. Then she pushed past him and stalked outside the hut.

He watched her go, unwilling to feel any guilt. No matter how vulnerable she appeared, no matter how expertly she plied her charms, he couldn't trust her again.

She'd devastated him before, crushing any illusions he had.

And he'd be damned if he'd let her make a fool of him twice.

Chapter 4

Her sandals rubbing her soles raw, Gabi limped down the rocky hillside, unable to believe how thoroughly she'd messed up. She'd failed to get that ring. She'd failed to get the intelligence she needed to finally bring down Ortiz. She had the police on her trail, the Americans suspecting her of murder. She'd even made Rafe suspicious of her—a disaster she didn't need.

He came into view on the slope below her, his wide shoulders padded with muscles, his thick, black hair gleaming in the morning mist. And an unsettled feeling slivered through her, a sharp, visceral awareness she'd been trying all night to ignore.

Rafe was the last person she could afford to be stuck with, but she didn't have much choice. The police would be watching her office. They'd stake out her family's ancestral estate, which she'd kept boarded up since she left País Vell. And fleeing the country would do no good with the Americans in pursuit.

Her only real recourse was to contact her father's cousin, the prime minister, who'd been in on her plan from the start. But she couldn't approach him directly. Ortiz would arrest her if she tried. And even the prime minister couldn't acquit her of the diplomat's murder without proof. As the right-hand man of the king, Ortiz had too much power.

She skirted a cluster of pine trees, trying not to panic at the debacle she'd made of the night. She had to calm down, retrieve that message she'd intercepted and prove her story to Rafe. Then somehow, she'd convince him to give her that ring.

Several yards later, the ground leveled out, the pine trees giving way to a lush green valley bisected by low stone walls. Rafe glanced back, and she abruptly straightened, refusing to let him see her limp. The problem was, she'd put on the performance of her life the night she'd dumped him, playing the part of a spoiled heiress to the hilt. But the same award-worthy act that had driven him away kept him from trusting her now.

She straggled to a halt beside him, determined to brazen it out. "What's wrong? Why did you stop?"

"We're nearly to the farmhouse." He gestured toward a cluster of small stone buildings, their tin roofs poking through the rising mist. "I'm going to look for a car. We'll never make it to town at this rate."

She grimaced, aware that she'd slowed their pace. "It's these sandals. They're giving me blisters. Maybe we can find some shoes in the house."

He quirked a brow. "You're not suggesting we steal them? An *aristocrat* like you?"

Her face warmed. She crossed her arms, knowing she deserved his contempt. But she couldn't tell him why she'd lied that night, no matter how much his derision hurt. She had to guard the truth with her life.

But surely they could manage a cease-fire, at least until they parted ways. "Listen, Rafe, about that night…"

"Forget it."

"But I didn't—"

"I said to forget it. You were clear enough back then. I don't need your excuses now."

Her belly twisted, his obvious resentment wobbling her heart. So much for forging a truce.

"I wasn't trying to make excuses. But since we're stuck together for awhile, I thought we could be civil at least."

"Civil?" he scoffed. "Sure. We can be civil—when you tell me why you're really here."

She hesitated. She wished she could reveal the entire story, but it was too dangerous for them both.

He let out an angry hiss. "That's what I thought."

"Rafe…"

"Forget it. Just wait here. I'll go look for some clothes."

Her pride stung, she raised her chin. "I can do it. I don't expect you to commit a crime for my sake."

"I'm not doing it to be nice. But I don't intend to get arrested because you screwed up."

"Fine." She didn't need his forgiveness. She hadn't wanted to hurt him, but she didn't regret what she'd done. She'd had no choice.

Still smarting, she pulled up the hem of her ball gown, and took out the cache of emergency cash she'd tucked into her thigh-high stocking's band. "Here. Leave them this." She held out a hundred euro bill. "It should cover anything you take."

His lips curled. He shot her a look of such utter disgust that she quickly lowered her hand. "Everything comes down to money for you, doesn't it?" he said. "That's always your bottom line."

"No. That's not true. I never—"

"Well, I don't need it. I never did, no matter what you and your father thought."

His eyes coldly furious, he turned, braced his hand on the crumbling stone wall, and vaulted into the yard. Then he ducked beneath a clothesline, scattering a flock of chickens as he stalked away.

Her heart stumbling, she watched him go. She deserved his scorn. She'd intentionally insulted his honor that night, hitting his most vulnerable spot. It had been the only way to drive him away.

In truth, she'd never cared about his lack of wealth. That had been her father's concern, the reason he'd tried to halt their teenage affair. But she couldn't fault her father for that. Rafe came from a criminal family. He had none of the breeding or wealth her protective, widowed father had wanted for his only child.

So she'd gone abroad to college at her father's request. He'd hoped the six years they'd spent apart would lessen her fascination with Rafe. But the more time passed, the more she respected the man he'd become. Rafe had worked his way out of poverty, making his fortune through grit and determination, defying society's low expectations of him. He'd tackled every obstacle, even resisting pressure from his family to resume his life of crime.

And her youthful infatuation had matured into something far more enduring—admiration and love.

She exhaled, pushing aside the painful memories. She couldn't dwell on the past. She had more important problems to worry about now—such as surviving Ortiz. Determined to keep her mind on track, she moved out of sight of the farmhouse, tucked the money back into her stocking, and settled in to wait for Rafe.

A rooster strutted past. The hollow clanking of cowbells came from the distant fields. A nuthatch landed on the old stone wall, then flitted over the barn.

"It's me," Rafe called a moment later, his deep voice emerging from the mist. He hopped back over the wall in an easy, effortless movement, a bundle tucked under his arm.

"That was fast."

"It's a small house." His eyes still cold, he handed her the rolled-up clothes. "The sizes are probably wrong, but they're better than what you have on."

Grateful, she shook out the bundle of typical country clothes—a pair of loose woolen leggings, a sleeveless, shiftlike top, and more importantly, some flat-soled, canvas shoes.

"These should work." She glanced around, looking for a place to change. Rafe leaned against the wall and crossed his arms.

Knowing she didn't have much claim to modesty after that striptease in the diplomat's bedroom, she turned her back to Rafe, kicked off her designer sandals and tugged the leggings on under her gown. Then she slipped off the sweater and evening gown, shivering in the crisp air, and pulled the sweater back on. She put the knee-length shift over the sweater and tied it at the waist, then added the woolen socks. The espadrilles were loose, but they beat her torturous shoes.

She spun back to Rafe. "How do I look?"

He frowned. "Do something with your hair. It doesn't match those clothes."

"Fine." Hurt by his indifference, she pulled the pins from her hair. "But in case you're wondering, you don't look like a farmer, either." He'd donned a *boina*, the black beret men in the Pyrenees Mountains typically wore. But with his arm muscles bulging, and the morning beard stubble darkening his granite jaw, he looked more like a *La Brigada* terrorist wielding a submachine gun than a farmer heading out to milk cows.

She plucked the rest of the pins from her hair and braided it in a simple style. Then she ripped a piece of lace off her tattered Balenciaga ballgown and used it to secure the end. "Is that better?" she challenged.

His gaze swung to hers. Several taut heartbeats ticked past. Something shifted in his obsidian eyes, the sudden intensity scrambling her pulse. Then he dropped his gaze, making a hot, slow slide over her breasts and legs, causing a rush of heat in her blood. And without warning, a long-buried sliver of excitement stirred inside her—a remnant of the daring girl she'd once been.

He abruptly straightened. "There's a car by the house. We can use it to get to town." He turned and strode away.

Shaken by her reaction, Gabi struggled to breathe. What had just happened? She never responded to men. *Never.* Ortiz had killed those feelings the night of that brutal attack.

Instead, she flirted. She teased. She used men's desires to create an illusion, calling on her years as an amateur actress to give the impression she was interested in them.

But it was an act, a ploy, a deliberate means to an end. It was a way to deflect their attention, to keep her true feelings hidden—enabling *her* to stay in control.

But Rafe was different. He wasn't like other men. He'd burrowed past her defenses, managing to unearth longings she had to keep buried, resurrecting yearnings in which she could never indulge.

And that scared her more than Ortiz.

The drive to town was torture. Like Pandora's box, once open, the feelings Rafe had evoked refused to go away, despite Gabi's efforts to keep them suppressed. She was far too conscious of the sexy beard stubble darkening his jaw, his broad shoulders crowding hers in the compact car, his knuckles grazing her leg every time he shifted gears.

By the time they left the two-lane highway and entered the medieval village of País Vell, she was relieved to turn her mind back to Ortiz. As she'd expected, police surrounded Rafe's apartment and gem shop. Ortiz's men stood guard at her corporate headquarters and the five-star hotel where she'd booked a room. More royal guards patrolled the village's winding streets, presumably to keep the peace during the G-6 summit—or hunt for them.

Rafe pulled the farmer's car to a stop on a narrow side street, keeping the motor running as he met her eyes. "We need to split up. It's the only way we can fool the guards. I'll ditch the car, then meet up with you after that."

Her stomach swooped. She'd wanted to get away

from Rafe, but not like this. Not with police swarming the village. Not with nowhere safe to hide. And not without that ring—the proof she needed to defeat Ortiz.

"Where do you want to meet?" she asked.

His forehead creased. "We'll have to use my family's hideout. It's the only place where I know that we'll be safe."

She shot him a startled glance. Rafe had never revealed the location of his family's safe house, not even when they were engaged. That he'd do so now showed just how desperate he believed their predicament was. "Where is it?"

"Go through the market." He angled his head toward the old stone building at the end of the cobblestoned street. "Take a left at the fish seller's stall, the one in the back by the loading bay. There's a maintenance closet at the end of the hallway. Wait for me there."

Still surprised that he'd confided in her, she skipped her gaze up the cobblestone street, past wrought iron balconies and lampposts, past ancient noble houses with escutcheons carved over their doors. At the entrance to the market stood a royal guard.

"All right," she agreed. She didn't have much choice.

Summoning her courage, she pushed the car door open—but Rafe touched her arm, and she stopped. His worried eyes met hers. "Be careful."

Sudden emotions crowded her throat, his unexpected concern bringing a spurt of warmth to her chest. "You, too." No matter how badly their relationship had ended, she didn't want to see him hurt.

He released her arm with a nod. She dragged in a breath and hopped out. Rafe made a U-turn and roared off, the car's tires clacking on the uneven stones.

The low whine of the engine faded. Alone now, she turned toward the guard. Two elderly women toddled past, pulling their shopping carts behind them, long, crusty loaves of bread peeking out of their bags.

Gabi closed her eyes, calling on her acting skills to play her part. Envisioning a modest farm girl, she hunched her shoulders and bowed her head, then shuffled toward the market, careful not to make eye contact with the royal guard.

Her pulse quickened as she neared the entrance. The armed guard turned her way, and her heart began to pound.

"*Oye.* You!" the guard called out. "Stop!"

Her throat went dust dry. She rushed up the steps, pretending she hadn't heard. "Stop!" he shouted again, but she slipped inside the market and merged with the bustling crowd.

Afraid running would attract his attention, she kept her pace to a rapid walk, hurrying as fast as she dared past fruit stands and barrels of olives, dodging garlic ropes hanging from hooks. Halfway down the crowded aisle, she braved a quick glance back, and her heart careened to a halt. *He was behind her.* She whipped around and swore.

Her palms dampened with sweat. Adrenaline shot through her veins, making it hard to think. She had to stay calm, act normal—and find a way to lose him in the jostling crowd.

Still weaving her way through the shoppers, she rounded the corner by a dairy case—but another guard blocked her path. Spinning around abruptly, she feigned interest in the wheels of cheese.

Her heart thundered fast. She tried frantically to form

a plan. She couldn't head to the fishmonger's stall and lead the danger to Rafe. But how could she escape the police?

A group of teenagers headed toward her, laughing and clowning around. Hoping the guards wouldn't shoot around children, she waited until they reached her, then merged with the boisterous group. They rounded another corner, headed up the produce aisle, and Gabi snuck another glance.

No sign of the guards. She broke free from the group and ran. Knowing she only had seconds, she darted though the milling shoppers, dodging a woman pushing a stroller, almost plowing down a grandmother with a wool scarf draped over her cart. Praying for forgiveness, she grabbed the scarf, ducked behind a stand of apples, and tied the cloth over her head.

Her cheeks flamed, Rafe's indignant words echoing in her mind. She could hardly claim the moral high ground now.

She peeked out from behind the apples. Neither guard was in sight. Her heart skipping in uneven beats, she rose and rushed to the fish seller's stall, nearly knocking over a table of trout. Then she took another swift glance back.

They still weren't there. Relief tumbling through her, she hung a left by the loading dock and searched the hallway for Rafe.

Suddenly a door swung open beside her. Rafe reached out and grabbed her arm. "What took you so long?" he demanded, pulling her inside. A dim bulb lit the cramped space.

The door clicked closed. Her pulse still chaotic she

sagged back against some brooms. "A couple of guards were following me."

His gaze sharpened on hers. "Did they see you come in here?"

"No, I lost them a few aisles back."

His frown deepened, his eyes revealing his mistrust. "Really," she assured him. "I'm sure they didn't see where I went."

He gave her a reluctant nod. "All right, then. Let's go."

He opened a door behind him and turned off the closet light. Gabi followed him up an ancient wooden staircase, the steps worn down from centuries of use. The pale light from a distant window revealed dust motes drifting in the musty air.

Three stories later, they reached the top. Gabi waited on the landing, breathing heavily, while Rafe unlocked the massive door. He motioned her inside, and she glanced around.

The Navarro family's safe house was an old interior apartment, the kind that housed the poorer citizens of País Vell. To the left was a tiny kitchen. To the right was a small parlor filled with mismatched, overstuffed chairs. A narrow hallway ran past the kitchen, flanked by several closed doors. The apartment's only windows overlooked a cement courtyard where the residents hung their wash.

Without warning, one of the bedroom doors swung open, and a man appeared in the hall. He stopped in his tracks, surprise flitting across his darkly handsome face as he looked her way.

Gabi's heart skipped several beats. This had to be Rafe's brother; he had the same black hair and chiseled cheeks, the same tall, wide-shouldered build. But when he shifted his gaze to Rafe, his expression hardened, stripped of any welcoming warmth.

"My brother Javier," Rafe confirmed, making the introductions.

Javier gave her a neutral nod, then returned his attention to Rafe, a cold smile slashing his face. "You were on the news," he said. "There's a reward out for your arrest."

A chill scuttling through her, Gabi crossed her arms. She'd expected as much from Ortiz. But hearing proof they were being hunted…

"We won't stay long," Rafe said, his own voice clipped. "We just need to use the computer."

"It's in the kitchen."

"I'll get started," she said quickly, unable to miss the animosity sparking between the men. Whatever the cause of their differences, they didn't need her to intrude.

She found the laptop on the kitchen table and turned it on. But her thoughts lingered on Rafe's family as she waited for it to boot up. She knew he had two younger brothers. She also knew they'd had a falling out twelve years ago when Rafe had left the family business, shortly after he'd met her.

But he'd never talked about his childhood in any detail, never discussed what it was like growing up in a family of thieves. He'd shown off his skills—opening locks, scaling impossible heights, thrilling her with his daring and nerve. But he'd never dwelled on the harsh reality of what it meant to be a criminal, leading her young, romantic imagination to glamorize their life.

But being here in their hideout made it impossible to

whitewash the truth. She scanned the scuffed linoleum floor, the peeling laminate countertops crammed with gemological supplies—microscopes, lamps, jewelry loupes and scales. These people were burglars. They broke into people's houses and stole jewels. There was nothing noble about what they did, no way to cast it in a sexy mystique.

Still, she'd learned one thing during her frenetic escape from Ortiz. Desperation influenced behavior. And it was far easier to condemn others for breaking the law when her own life wasn't at stake.

Turning her thoughts from Rafe—and back to the police chief—she typed in the URL for the FerrCom corporate website and entered her password, then waited for it to load. A second later the front door thudded closed, and Rafe strode into the room. "You want something to drink?" he asked. "Soda? Water? Beer or wine?"

"Water's fine."

He took two plastic bottles from the refrigerator, set one on the table for her, and unscrewed the cap on his. Then he took several deep gulps, his Adam's apple dipping in his heavily whiskered throat.

She skimmed the angles of his unshaven jaw, the roped muscles in his corded arms, the impressive width of his rock-hard chest. And suddenly, that edgy, restless feeling thrummed inside her, the same sensual awareness she'd experienced in the farmer's field.

Alarmed at the direction of her thoughts, she tore her gaze away. "You and your brother don't seem to get along."

He wiped his mouth on the back of his hand and let out a bitter laugh. "Yeah, you could say that. Good thing he hates Ortiz more than me, or he'd collect on that reward."

She shot him a startled glance. "You can't mean that."

"The hell I don't." He hooked a chair by its leg and sat. "This is the first time he's talked to me in years."

Shocked, she searched his eyes. "Why? Because you quit the family business?"

"Pretty much."

"But that's ridiculous. How can he hold that against you after all this time?" That was a dozen years ago. And why would he care what Rafe did?

Rafe took another long swallow of water, then gave her a thoughtful look, as if debating whether to tell her more.

She dragged her gaze to her water, hurt by his reluctance to tell her—which made no sense. Rafe didn't owe her any explanations. He had no reason to reveal his family secrets to her. She'd forfeited that right long ago.

But then he released his breath. "It wasn't just that. When you were going to school in the states my father got it into his head to rob the casino. He asked me to help him, and I refused." He lifted one broad shoulder in a shrug. "It went as badly as I expected, and he got caught."

Her heart wobbled hard. Beneath his matter-of-fact recital, she sensed a wealth of pain. "How come you didn't help him?"

He polished off the water, then tapped the empty plastic bottle on the chair. "It was too risky, for one thing. The only person who's ever done it is a guy named Dante Quevedo—assuming the rumors about him are true. I tried to convince my father of that, but he insisted we could pull it off."

"So he made a bad choice."

Rafe shrugged. "Every job has risks, and this one had more than most. But he was obsessed with the idea and couldn't let it go. It was more about the challenge than the loot."

She could understand that. She'd been equally as obsessed for the past three years with bringing down Ortiz. "I still don't see why they blamed you. They couldn't expect you to risk your life."

A bitter smile edged his mouth. "We're a family. They expected me to help him, no matter what."

And then they'd blamed Rafe when his father had failed.

"I see," she said, because for the first time she really did. She understood the courage it had taken to break with his family, the depths of the sacrifice he'd made to give up their lifestyle—a decision his family still hadn't forgiven after all these years.

"And the other reason?" she asked, her voice uneven. "You said there was more than one reason you'd refused."

His eyes connected with hers. "I'd promised you I'd go straight, and *I* don't go back on my word."

Unlike her.

Her face burned. She dropped her gaze to the computer screen, her belly roiling with guilt. No wonder Rafe despised her. He'd broken with his family for her sake. He'd refused to help his father so he could become a man she'd respect. And she'd repaid him by insulting his honor and betraying his trust.

Stricken, she closed her eyes. She deserved his contempt. She'd hurt him in the worst possible way. But she couldn't explain, couldn't reveal why she'd had to lie. She could only work to bring down Ortiz, the man who'd destroyed their lives.

Still unable to bear Rafe's censure, she forced her attention back to the task at hand. She scrolled through the diplomat's records, trying to ignore Rafe sitting beside her, his perceptive gaze monitoring her moves.

But the message wasn't there.

Her heart missed a beat.

Focus, she lectured herself sternly. She couldn't afford a distraction with everything she had at stake. Sitting up straighter, she began combing through the calls again.

But as she paged carefully through the records, a terrible feeling of dread burrowed inside. And by the time she'd reached the end, she couldn't ignore the truth. That call had disappeared.

And with it went her only proof.

"What's wrong?" Rafe asked.

Suddenly feeling dizzy, she met his eyes. "The message is gone."

"Gone *how?*"

She shook her head. "It's just…not there."

"What does that mean?"

"I don't know." Her stomach churning, she motioned toward the screen. "I can't explain it. It has to be there. There's no way it got erased."

"Then where is it?"

"I have no idea." Anxiety gurgled inside her. "It just disappeared."

He cocked a brow, his skepticism clear.

She didn't blame him for having doubts. Her story

sounded fake, even to her. "I'm telling you the truth, Rafe. I swear it. I intercepted that call, and now it's not there. I really didn't make this up."

"Right." He tipped back his chair, balancing on the back legs, his gaze never wavering from hers. "Then what happened?"

"I don't know. Maybe someone hacked into the system. But even if they did, they couldn't erase that file. We've got too many backup systems in place. Unless…"

Her mind raced. The tumult in her belly grew. "Unless they renamed it. They could have buried it in the archives by saving it as another file. We've got thousands of accounts. We'd never find it that way."

And with both the call and the intelligence missing, she had no way to fight Ortiz—while he had the entire world hunting for *her*.

"It had to be Ortiz," she said, feeling sick. "He has to be the traitor. But I can't prove it, unless that ring is connected somehow."

Rafe straightened his chair with a thump. "Forget it. I'm not giving up that ring."

"But you have to. It might be our only proof."

"I don't *have* to do a damned thing."

"But Ortiz is a murderer. A traitor. I can't believe you won't help."

"Believe it. He hired me to get that ring, and I'm not going back on my word."

Incredulous, she stared back. It didn't make sense. Rafe despised Ortiz. The police chief had persecuted his family for years. And there was no way he could work for a murderer, no matter how many years had passed. Rafe couldn't have changed that much.

"If it's money you need, I'll pay you—"

"I don't want your money. Why can't you get that through your head?"

"Then what *do* you want?" He didn't answer, and her desperation grew. "For God's sake, Rafe. You know what Ortiz is like. How can you possibly work for him?"

"I told you. It's personal."

"He's trying to kill us. You can't *get* more personal than that."

Rafe shoved away from the table. He strode to the tiny window and stared through the dirty glass, tension permeating his unyielding stance.

Gabi frowned, stunned by his reaction, unable to make sense of it all. Rafe was loyal, principled. He'd even refused to help his father rather than break his solemn vow.

So why had he broken it for Ortiz? What hold could the police chief possibly have over him?

Her mind whirled from Rafe's brother Javier, to his vow to go straight, to his family's grudge against him...

All of a sudden, she understood. "Oh, God," she breathed. "It's your father, isn't it? That's why you took this job."

Rafe didn't move. For a minute she thought he hadn't heard. But then his broad shoulders slumped, and he turned around to face her, his tortured eyes confirming her fear. "Ortiz agreed to release him if I got that ring."

"But—"

"He has cancer." The bleakness in his voice barreled through her, gutting her heart. "He only has a few more weeks to live. And for once in my life, I can't let him down."

Chapter 5

Gabi stared at Rafe across the kitchen, the enormity of his revelation upending her world. His father was dying in prison. Rafe needed the ring to free him. He couldn't let the dying man down.

Then she caught the guilt flickering in his tortured eyes, and an even worse realization kicked her straight in the heart. It wasn't just Rafe's family who blamed him for his father's arrest. *He blamed himself.*

She pressed her hand to her lips, the insight making her reel. This was more than just a chance to free his father. This was Rafe's one chance for redemption, to finally gain his family's forgiveness and atone for his mistakes.

And suddenly, it all made sense. His bargain with Ortiz. His willingness to risk his life and break his vow. His refusal to give up that ring.

"It wasn't your fault he got arrested," she said, her

heart racing. His gaze angled away, and she leaned forward, needing him to understand. "I mean it, Rafe. You can't seriously blame yourself for what he did."

"He's my father. I should have helped him. My family was right about that."

"But you'd reformed. They were wrong to ask you to break your word. That wasn't fair to you. And what if you *had* helped him? You probably would have both gotten caught. You said there was no way to pull it off."

"Maybe." He grimaced and shook his head. "That's something I'll never know. But it doesn't change the fact that I need to free him now."

She experienced a spurt of dread. "Even if it means we can't convict Ortiz?"

"Even then."

"But—"

"You don't understand." He strode back to the table and gripped the chair, his black eyes turning intense. "You've never been locked up."

"That's true, but—"

"There's no *but* about it. You have no idea what it's like to live in a cage, stripped of your freedom, your dignity. How inhuman it is. Degrading. And I can't let him die like that—like some kind of animal. Especially if it's my fault he's there."

She swallowed hard, unable to miss the misery in his voice. But he was wrong. She *did* understand. She'd suffered that same humiliation, that same degradation and vulnerability at the hands of Ortiz.

She looked away, trying to block out the sight of Rafe's tortured eyes—but it didn't help. And she knew right then that she couldn't stop him. She had no right to stand in his way. She'd already caused him enough pain.

But if he used that ring to free his father, it would deprive her of the justice *she* craved. And she couldn't forfeit her goal! She'd worked three long years toward this moment. Now she finally had the chance to bring down Ortiz—the vile traitor who'd ruined her life.

But then what could she do about Rafe?

A dull throb formed between her brows. She rubbed at the ache, trying to sort through her muddled thoughts. They both needed that ring, but for different reasons. How could she reconcile their opposing needs?

She exhaled. "What a mess."

Rafe grunted his agreement. Then he crossed the room to the counter, pulled the velvet pouch from his pocket, and dumped the gold ring into his palm.

"What are you doing?" she asked.

"Finding out what we're dealing with here." He put the ring into a gadget the size of a fax machine and turned it on.

While he worked, she slumped back in her chair, still trying to find a way to satisfy both their needs. But one thing was clear. She couldn't, in good conscience, take that ring and deny Rafe the absolution he sought. It wasn't fair to him.

But if it had a connection to her case...

"So what do you think of the ring?" she asked.

He turned off the machine. "The purity of the gold checks out." He carted a microscope to the table and plugged it in, then pulled up a chair and sat.

Her mind still in turmoil, she watched him inspect the ring, his dark brows furrowed in concentration, the low light intensifying the blue undertones in his straight black hair. He made an adjustment to the eyepiece, his lean, callused fingers working the knobs with expert ease. She skimmed the sexy slant of his cheekbones, the heavy razor stubble covering his jaw, the short hairs at the nape of his neck.

She wondered how many hours she'd spent like this—studying his face, his jaw, his arms, admiring the dexterity of his fingers, the way the sunlight glinted off his hair. Enthralled with his mind and skill.

And suddenly, out of nowhere, more memories came spinning back. His black eyes burning with hunger. His body taut with arousal. The untamed urgency of his kiss. Her own body naked, shuddering with ecstasy, as he drove inside her, shattering her with bliss.

Her pulse ragged, she dragged her gaze away. She'd adored this man. She'd loved his wildness, his daring, his nerve. And when he'd taken her in his arms...

He'd been unlike any man she'd ever met. He'd challenged her to test her limits, stoking her need for adventure, urging her to break past her inhibitions and live.

She eased out a weary sigh. She'd loved him, all right. Even the six years they'd spent apart during college hadn't lessened his appeal. If anything, she'd come to respect his achievements more. And it had killed her to give him up.

But Ortiz had demolished her world the night of that attack. He'd ripped away her security, destroying her faith in authority, her belief in the goodness of men.

He'd tried to take her life—and failed. But he'd stolen her future with Rafe. And he'd robbed her of the ability to dream. Thanks to Ortiz, she no longer indulged in wishful thinking. She no longer believed in happily-ever-afters or other fantasies.

Now she stayed firmly rooted in reality, focusing only on what mattered most—justice. Survival.

Revenge.

Still, sitting here with the man she'd once loved, it was hard not to remember the good times.

Or yearn for a life she could never have.

Shaking her head at her foolish thoughts, she returned her focus to the ring. "So what's the verdict?"

Rafe didn't look up. "It's real."

"How can you tell?"

He snapped off the microscope and extracted the ring, then hefted it in his palm. "Everything about it feels right. The density, the weight. The royal mark dates from the seventeenth century, the time of the last queen. The Latin inscription matches, too. *Morior invictus.* If it's a copy, it's a damned good one."

She frowned at the ring, its pure gold gleaming with hidden fire. She didn't doubt Rafe's assessment. If anyone knew jewelry, it was him. Not only did he come from a long line of jewel thieves, but he'd earned a degree in gemology. He'd even founded a business dealing in precious gems.

"Could something be hidden in the ring?" she asked.

"Like a microchip?" Amusement played around his mouth. "I doubt it. There are still traces of wax in the crevices from when it was used as a royal seal, and a layer of dust over that. If someone tampered with the setting, they did a remarkable job covering it up."

Disappointed, Gabi rose and went to the window. She braced her hands on the rotting sill and stared down at the web of clotheslines, unable to escape the irony. Rafe had solved her dilemma. If that signet ring was authentic—as he believed—she had no claim on it. He might as well use it to bargain for his father's release—if he dared to risk arrest.

But that left her in dire straits. The diplomat was dead. Ortiz had surely confiscated the intelligence that would expose his traitorous ties. Even the telephone message she'd intercepted had disappeared. She had no way to prove her innocence in the American diplomat's murder, no way to incriminate the police chief in her father's death. And authorities worldwide were hunting her down.

Shaken, she rubbed her arms, determined to figure a way out of this trap. Ortiz *must* have the intelligence by now. He would have found it in the diplomat's bedroom—either when he killed him or later, when he "investigated" the crime. And he'd want to destroy it fast, before anyone got wind of what it contained.

Anxiety threatened to overwhelm her, but she stomped it back. She couldn't panic. Not yet. She had to assume the intelligence still existed—at least for now. But neither could she waste time. With every passing moment the chances that he'd destroyed it grew.

Rafe rose and returned the microscope to the counter. She eyed his fluid movements, experiencing a twist of regret—which made no sense. She was happy he could free his father. And she should be glad to get away from him. He disrupted her equilibrium, threatening to expose secrets she couldn't reveal. So why the sudden reluctance to part ways?

Shaking off her doubts, she cleared her throat. "Listen, Rafe. If you're right about that ring, then it has nothing to do with me. You might as well hand it over to Ortiz."

His dark brows gathering, he leaned back against the counter and crossed his arms. "What are you going to do?"

"Leave. Find that missing intelligence."

"How do you plan to do that?"

God only knew. "Ortiz probably took it from the diplomat's bedroom. I'm sure he'll want to destroy it, so he won't let it out of his sight. And since he had a late night searching for us, he's probably still at home. So I'll start looking there, at his house in town."

He shot her a look of disbelief. "Are you nuts? You can't break into his place. You'll never make it out alive."

A stark chill shivered through her. If Ortiz caught her, killing her was the least of the horrors he could inflict. "You have a better suggestion?"

"Yeah, that you forget it."

"I can't. I told you he murdered my father. There's no way I'm giving up until he's behind bars."

"So you're going to risk your life?"

"My life's already at risk. You heard your brother— Ortiz has a reward out for our capture. He's searching for us right now. Or have you forgotten that?"

"Forgotten?" His mouth thinned. A flush darkened the rugged planes of his face. He strode toward her across the room, his steps deliberate, stopping so close she could see the pulse ticking in his granite jaw, the barely banked fury blazing in his coal-black eyes.

"I haven't forgotten anything," he growled. And for one crazy moment, she wasn't sure if he meant Ortiz, her betrayal—or the ecstasy they'd shared.

His gaze stayed clamped on hers, and the stark intensity touched off something inside her, half-forgotten cravings she'd worked so hard to repress. She tried to step back, to break the spell before he got too close— or she did something she'd regret. But he reached out and cupped her jaw, his warm, rough hand jolting her senses, sending erotic sparks racing over her skin.

Her throat turned bone dry. She abruptly lost the ability to breathe. Then his thumb blazed a path down the skin of her throat, shooting fiery heat straight to her loins. And hunger fisted inside her, raw and sharp and deep, urging her to step into his arms, to seize the moment and soar.

She struggled to recover her senses. But his hungry eyes held her immobile, so black and mesmerizing and hot that she couldn't tear her gaze away. And unguarded yearnings surged inside her, making her ache to reach out and stroke his face, to press her body against his, and be the carefree girl he'd known.

But then her palms began to sweat. Her pulse took flight, tapping a frenzied beat in her throat. Shivers invaded her limbs, a tight, suffocated feeling squeezing her constricted lungs of air.

She closed her eyes, trying desperately to stay in control. *Not this. Not now!* She inhaled deeply, struggling to regulate her breath the way the counselor had taught her, and stave off the billowing fear. But it was no use. Rafe was too close. Too big. *Too male.*

Nausea rose inside her. Her frantic heart bludgeoned her chest. She jerked from his grasp and whirled around, then pressed her palms to the glass. Gulping in air, she battled to regain her equilibrium, despising the hold Ortiz still had on her after all this time.

Several seconds passed. Her pulse slowed to a steady beat. Gathering the remnants of her tattered composure, she tried to assume her seductress act, to take refuge in the jaded, worldly role she played to hide the lurking fear.

But her usual resources failed her. She simply couldn't pretend around Rafe. Praying he hadn't noticed her bizarre reaction, that he'd attribute her abrupt withdrawal to something—anything—else, she forced herself to turn around.

He'd noticed. Speculation brewed in his narrowed eyes.

Needing to avoid his questions at any cost, she raised her chin. "I don't expect you to come with me. Whatever I do isn't your business now."

"And I told you. We're in this thing together. You're not going to Ortiz's place alone."

Relief swept through her. Rafe was willing to help her. She didn't have to face Ortiz alone—which comforted her more than she cared to admit. "Does that mean you trust me?"

"Trust you?" He barked out a cynical laugh. "Don't stretch it. I'm not that big a fool." His eyes still angry, he turned on his heel and stalked off.

Gabi staggered to a chair and sat, the encounter leaving her badly unnerved. What was happening to her? She'd spent three years suppressing those memories about Ortiz. Three years keeping a lid on the terror and concealing the dreadful past.

And now, in a few short hours, Rafe had battered through her defenses, rendering her unable to act the seductress, eliciting a host of dangerous emotions—panic, fear, desire.

Hysteria burbled inside her, the irony hitting her hard. Whether Rafe trusted her or not no longer mattered. She now had a much greater threat to contend with.

She couldn't trust herself.

* * *

Rafe had lied. He was the biggest fool on earth. His response to Gabrielle proved that.

Still incredulous over his reaction to her, he strode down the narrow hall. One look at those amber eyes and he forgot her lies, forgot that she'd betrayed him, forgot that the vulnerable look she wielded was only a well-rehearsed act.

Hell, he'd nearly given in to the urge to kiss her, making him as brainless as that diplomat—panting at her feet while she led him on.

And she'd clearly tried to manipulate him. The way she'd gone from hot to cold demonstrated that. She changed moods faster than he could blink—and none of them were sincere. But for some unfathomable reason whenever he got near her, his mind clicked off. She suckered him in, and he fell for it every time.

He entered the bedroom and kicked the door shut, hoping the solitude would help him regain some sense. By rights he should let her leave. He didn't believe her story. Her proof—that message—had conveniently disappeared. And he knew she was withholding important information. She might be a skilled actress, but he'd spent years studying every nuance of her expressions and knew that she hadn't come clean.

But even though it rankled, he was stuck with her for now. Because the fact was, he trusted the police chief even less than he did her. And once he handed Ortiz that ring, there was nothing to keep him from reneging on their deal. It would be just like Ortiz to arrest him for the diplomat's murder *and* keep his father in jail.

Which meant he needed a bargaining chip, something to force the police chief to hold up his end of the agreement—like that missing intelligence.

Assuming Gabi had told him the truth and it was real.

And what were the chances of that?

Swearing at his predicament, he crossed the room to the armoire and scanned the racks of clothes. He pulled on a dark blue T-shirt, scooped up a small backpack, and tossed in a flashlight and tools.

Still disgusted at his reaction, he closed the armoire, then caught his reflection in the mirror and scowled. He'd lost his mind, all right. Bad enough that he'd broken his vow, throwing away a dozen years of good behavior to make that pact with Ortiz. Worse, he'd fallen in with Gabrielle, a woman he couldn't trust. And now he was going to sneak into Ortiz's palace, a mission so fraught with danger that even his family had never tried.

He thinned his lips. He might be a bloody fool, but he hadn't come this far to fail. And no matter what game Gabi was playing, he intended to win.

But an hour later, as he sat with Gabi on a small wooden bench in the *Plaza Mayor*, he was even more convinced that he'd gone insane. Pretending to be tourists, armed with maps, hats, cameras and munching sandwiches, they surreptitiously studied Ortiz's palace, which formed one corner of the medieval square.

Armed guards stood watch on the street outside the compound. More police secured the prime minister's office, a converted sixteenth century monastery that comprised one of the plaza's walls. In the center of the square, workmen hammered away, building a stage for the king's appearance, scheduled for the end of the G-6 summit in two days' time.

"So what do you think?" Gabi asked, her voice low.

Rafe tossed a bread crumb to some pigeons and shook his head. "It's suicidal." It would be hard enough to break in during normal times, but with the king scheduled to give that speech, Ortiz had ramped the security up.

"There has to be a way in," she argued.

He polished off his sandwich and met her eyes. She'd changed into a T-shirt and jeans one of his brother's cohorts had left behind. With her face freshly scrubbed of makeup, her hair pulled back in a ponytail, she looked younger, less elegant, enabling them to hide in plain sight.

"You have a suggestion?" he asked.

Her forehead creased. She shifted her gaze to Ortiz's palace and nibbled her bottom lip. "Not really, but we have to get in there. The longer we wait, the greater the chance he'll destroy that evidence."

And the greater their odds of arrest. Between Ortiz's royal guards and the Americans' formidable resources, they didn't stand a chance of evading capture for long.

But how could they break in?

He swung his gaze back to the palace, reviewing what he knew of the place. It was a typical medieval structure built around a central courtyard and hidden behind stone walls, making reconnaissance hard.

"We don't only have to get past the guards," he pointed out. "He probably has a security system we haven't checked out." Which only intensified his misgivings about this attempt. Back when he was a professional thief, he'd scrupulously followed two rules. First off, he'd planned each heist in painstaking detail, to minimize surprises that could trip him up. If he wasn't convinced he could escape detection, he called off the mission.

And he'd always worked alone. Partners made mistakes, increasing the chance of arrest—and he refused to entrust his precious freedom to anyone else.

Those were the ironclad rules he'd lived by, the two inviolate laws that had enabled him to survive.

But now, thanks to Gabrielle, he was about to break them both.

"At least he won't be expecting us," she said. "We have the advantage of surprise."

"That's not much to go on." He rummaged in the backpack, retrieving the plastic bottle they'd brought. "You want more water?"

She shook her head, so he finished it off and tossed it in a nearby bin. He grabbed a map, pretending to study it as he scanned the narrow, cobblestone street, the palace's red tiled roof, the ancient royal insignia carved into the stones above the wooden door. Behind the palace, the Roman aqueduct towered over the town.

Rafe's gaze stalled on the aqueduct, and he frowned. "This part of town was built over the original Roman settlement, right?"

Gabi turned her head. "I guess so. Why?"

"What do you know about Roman engineering?"

"Not much. Just that they built a lot of roads and bridges."

"Exactly. They were great engineers." A sudden idea brewing, he skipped his gaze from the aqueduct to Ortiz's palace, then back to the tourist map.

"So what's your point?" she asked.

"They planned their cities. And one of the things they worried about was drainage." He gestured toward the narrow lane that ran to the edge of town. "These cobblestone streets came later, during medieval times. But I'd bet anything they were built on top of the old roads—which means they drain into the Roman sewers that tunnel under the town."

Her gaze snapped to his. "You want to crawl through the sewers?"

The horror in her voice made his mouth tick up. "You have a problem with that?"

"Yes. What if there are rats?"

"It won't be that bad."

"How do you know? Have you been in them?"

"No," he admitted, conceding the point. "I'm not even sure where they go."

Her eyes searched his. "But you think we can enter the palace that way?"

"That palace is one of the oldest structures in town. It even abuts the medieval wall, or what's left of it. My guess is it connects to the Roman sewer line, too."

She glanced back at the palace and gnawed her lip. "Supposing we decide to try it... How can we get inside the sewer?"

"Where it comes out. At the river." He rose and held out his hand. "It's the best bet we have right now."

She hesitated, her reluctance clear. But then a familiar glint entered her eyes, that same irrepressible spirit, that same unflagging determination that had originally won his heart. And for a moment, the years peeled away, and they were partners in adventure, up for any challenge, two teenagers crazy in love. She gripped his hand and rose.

Disgusted by his reaction, he turned away. What was the matter with him? His life was at stake. He had to get his father free. This wasn't the time to forget the armed guards, the dead diplomat. *Gabrielle's lies.*

But as he headed down the street toward the river, he realized he had a problem. Because instead of the conniving socialite who'd dumped him, he kept glimpsing the old Gabrielle, the gutsy woman he'd loved.

A woman he'd have to fight like hell to resist.

Chapter 6

Gabi was still trying to subdue her unruly emotions as she hiked behind Rafe down the narrow sidewalk, heading toward the river outside town. She'd finally recovered from that flashback in the kitchen. She'd even managed to ignore the erotic memories that kept bombarding her mind.

But what disturbed her most was the stark realization that everything she'd seen of Rafe so far—that he'd helped her escape the castle, that he'd risked his life to free his father, that he was willing to search for the missing intelligence, despite her lack of proof—demonstrated why she'd loved this man.

And that had her running scared. Because it was too darned dangerous to let herself like Rafe. It tempted her to let down her guard, to confide in him about the past, to beg him to forgive her for the terrible pain she'd caused.

But there was no way she could tell him the truth. Revealing that would jeopardize them both. So no matter how much he appealed to her, no matter how guilty she felt for the lies she'd told, she had to keep her mind on her job. She had to find the proof she needed to convict Ortiz and then hightail it away from Rafe—before she let something vital slip.

It didn't help that his strong shoulders filled her vision, that every time he turned his head, she glimpsed his virile, masculine profile, the sexy angle of his unshaven jaw....

Exasperated, she rolled her eyes. Determined to conquer this unruly obsession, she hurried to keep pace with his rapid strides. She rushed past a tiny bakery, then went by a bustling bar.

"...these two people," the police chief's voice boomed from the doorway.

Startled, Gabi stopped and spun around. She whipped her gaze up the winding street—but no one was there. Only an elderly woman dressed in widow's weeds hobbled into a house a block away.

But Gabi hadn't imagined that voice.

Her pulse accelerating, she backed up and peeked through the window of the bar. A television hung in the corner, Ortiz gazing out from the screen.

Her stomach went into a free fall at the sight of his cruel eyes. He stood in the dark by the roadblock, police lights flashing in the background—footage from the previous night.

"They're armed and dangerous," he continued, his sinister voice chilling her blood. "They shot the victim at point blank range. Anyone who spots them should notify us at once."

"Any idea of the motive?" a reporter asked from off-screen.

"Not yet," he answered, blinking as a flurry of flashbulbs went off. "But I promise you, we're doing everything possible to find them. We have the full cooperation of the French and Spanish governments, and the Americans have contributed resources, as well. We're also offering a reward for any information leading to their capture—half a million euros. We won't rest until justice is served."

Justice? Gabi hiccupped a bitter laugh. They'd have justice when *he* was locked behind bars.

The clinking of glasses jerked her back to awareness. She stepped away from the window, but could still see the television angled through the open door. The screen cut to a female newscaster, Rafe's mug shot pasted on her left. Below Rafe was a photo of Gabi and her father at a charity ball.

Her throat turned thick, an awful tightness gripping her chest at the sight of her father in his tuxedo, his gentle eyes smiling at her. She remembered that night. It was the last public event they'd attended before he'd died.

"Gabrielle Ferrer is a well-known socialite," the newscaster read while Gabi blinked back a sting of tears. "She took the helm of her father's corporation—FerrCom, S.A.—after he was killed in a robbery three years ago. She has a history with Rafael Navarro, who comes from a notorious crime family. It's believed they joined forces as teenagers, and that this current crime spree…"

Crime spree? Gabi glared at the newscaster. Talk about distorting the facts!

Outraged, she turned to Rafe. But he'd already made it to the two-lane highway at the end of the cobblestone street. She broke into a jog to catch up.

"We were just on television," she told him, breathless, as they crossed the road. "They're making us out to be Bonnie and Clyde. Only we're the jewel thief and the socialite."

He grunted. "The tabloids will love that."

He was right. Her heart plummeted as they headed toward the woods. This case had all the elements of intrigue—a murdered diplomat, her family's wealth, Rafe's criminal background—not to mention that reward. The media would cover the case unceasingly, making it impossible for them to escape scrutiny. How on earth were they going to hide?

Feeling even more uneasy, she swiveled to check behind them, relieved not to see the police. Still, she kept scanning their surroundings as she hiked beside Rafe through the woods.

They reached the river moments later and continued along the bank. The water gurgled past in the morning sunshine. Sparrows chirped from a thicket of berries close by. Beech trees fluttered in the gentle breeze, their yellow leaves bright amid the blue-green willows and firs.

But the peaceful scene did nothing to calm her nerves—because if she'd needed a reminder about the danger they faced, that newscast had done the trick.

"There it is," Rafe said.

She shielded her eyes from the sun and scanned the bank. "Where? I don't see anything."

"Down here." He leaped down the six-foot embankment, the metal tools in his backpack clanking as he landed on the rocks. She worked her way down slowly, climbing carefully over piles of deadfall to where he stood.

The tunnel was small, roughly six feet high and four feet wide, and topped with a Roman arch. A metal gate barricaded the entrance. Above the gate, the stones bore the Roman inscription "SPQR."

"Senatus Populusque Romanus," she recited. "The Senate and People of Rome." The abbreviation they'd used to identify their public works. She eyed the padlock on the gate. "Can you pick the lock?" she asked Rafe.

"It's too corroded. I'll have to cut it off." He swung down his backpack, took some bolt cutters from the bag, and got to work. Still jumpy after that newscast, Gabi ran her gaze along the opposite bank. But they seemed to be alone—so far.

The lock fell to the rocks, the sudden noise startling a flock of birds into flight. Rafe unwound the chain and set it aside, then opened the rusty gate.

Gabi peered at the inky water, wrinkling her nose at the fetid smell. "How deep do you think it is?"

"I'll find out." He returned the bolt cutter to his pack, picked up a nearby branch and used it to probe the depth. "A foot or two." His eyes met hers. "Are you okay with this? You can wait here if you want."

A sliver of warmth slid through her, that he'd cared enough to ask. "I'll be fine. A little water won't hurt me." Or whatever that substance was.

Approval flickered in his eyes, doing unwanted things to her insides. But then he stepped into the tunnel. The water came up to his knees. "It's cold," he warned.

Bracing herself, she ducked her head and waded in,

the frigid water jolting her nerves. At least she hoped it was water. She didn't dare think of what else it could be.

Ignoring the foul odor, she followed Rafe deeper into the tunnel, careful of her footing on the slippery rocks. The dank air filled her lungs. The sunlight dimmed as they hiked along. Rafe pulled a flashlight from his backpack, and the beam bounced over the square-cut stones.

They walked for a while in silence. Rafe probed the floor with his stick, the thumps muffled as he tapped the rocks. The water pushed past, the current surprisingly strong, turning her feet from cold to numb.

To keep her mind off her discomfort, she steered her thoughts back to Ortiz. She understood the police chief's strategy. He'd sent Rafe to the diplomat's bedroom to steal that ring under the guise of preventing civil unrest. In reality Ortiz had intended to arrest him, part of his personal vendetta against Rafe's family, which had eluded his capture for years.

That much seemed clear. His attack on her seemed murkier, but she thought she'd figured it out. Ortiz must have known she would be at the gala. He would have vetted the guest list and spotted her name. He couldn't have suspected her motives, but once she'd left the reception with the diplomat, he'd probably figured it out. And he'd seized the chance to kill her, finishing the job he'd begun years ago.

She shivered hard, the memory of that night icing her veins. He'd worn a mask when he'd murdered her father, an effective disguise. But he'd spoken to her when he'd tried to kill her, and she'd recognized his voice.

He'd left her for dead, never expecting her to survive.

But when she had—and didn't denounce him as her father's murderer—he must have assumed his disguise had worked. But now that she'd returned to País Vell, he couldn't take the chance that she'd identify him.

And she had to give him credit. The odds were that he'd succeed. He'd framed them for the diplomat's murder. He'd turned the citizens of País Vell into vigilantes by offering that huge reward. He'd even launched an international manhunt, which meant they couldn't evade capture for long. And once he had them in custody, he could easily arrange their deaths.

"What I don't understand is Arturo Menendez's reaction to all this," she said.

Rafe ducked his head and glanced back, the flashlight's beam heightening the hollows of his cheeks. "The prime minister?"

She nodded. "He knows why I attended the reception. I was the one who notified him about that intelligence, and we both agreed on the plan. So why isn't he defending us? Why is he letting Ortiz blame us for the crime?"

"Maybe he doesn't want to tip off the police chief."

That made sense. As the head of the king's security, Ortiz had formidable power. Menendez wouldn't want him to know they were onto him until they could present the king with proof.

"How much do you trust the prime minister?" Rafe asked as he started walking again.

Considering that, she frowned. Three years ago, she wouldn't have hesitated to endorse him. But since the attack she'd become more jaded, her faith in authority gone. Still…

"I've known him all my life. He's my father's first

cousin. He's ambitious, a typical politician in a lot of ways, but I think he cares about the country."

"Then he's loyal to the king?"

"Yes, definitely." Her voice echoed against the stones. "The spy ring he heads proves that." And he'd built his reputation on his fiercely pro-monarchist stance.

"Either way, I don't pose any threat to him. In fact, I'm helping him root out a traitor, which should benefit his career. So yes, I trust him." As much as she trusted anyone in this situation besides Rafe.

Rafe stooped to accommodate the low head room, his broad shoulders filling the narrow space. And she realized it was true. She did trust Rafe. She knew he would never hurt her, despite the way she'd treated him. He had an unshakable core of integrity, the same inner strength that had enabled him to stand against his family—one of the qualities she'd most loved.

While she'd brought him nothing but pain.

Guilt reared up, the terrible hurt she'd caused him becoming harder to ignore. "I'm sorry if I've messed things up for your father," she said.

Rafe stopped, turning slightly to meet her eyes. "You haven't. I doubt Ortiz ever intended to release him."

"Maybe not, but I'm sure I haven't helped." She paused, hoping he believed her. "I really am sorry about that."

His gaze stayed on hers for several heartbeats. Then his eyes softened fractionally, and he nodded, as if accepting the unspoken truce. It didn't change the past. It didn't solve the problems they still faced. But it was a start.

He cleared his throat, then aimed the flashlight at her legs. "Are you doing all right?"

"I'm fine, just freezing."

"We don't have far to go."

"How do you know?"

He swung around and resumed walking, the water glistening like oil in the flashlight's beam. "I counted off our paces down the road. As long as the sewer stays close to the course the street took, I should be able to get us there."

Her admiration went up another notch. It hadn't occurred to her to measure the distance to Ortiz's house. But that was typical of Rafe, always planning ahead. "How are we going to get out once we get there?"

"There should be an opening somewhere under the house. Like that one." He directed the light to a stone circle above their heads. "As long as they haven't cemented it shut."

Gabi frowned at that. They could probably chisel or saw through a barrier, assuming Rafe had the tools. But the noise would alert the guards. And if they failed to get into the palace...

She cut off that line of thought. They'd get in. They had to. This could be their only chance.

The sewer continued sloping uphill. She pushed against the current, her breathing growing labored, the slimy stones adding to the effort to stay erect. Her teeth chattered from the musty cold.

Several minutes later, the sound of rushing water increased. "What's that?" she asked, raising her voice above the noise.

Rafe's light skipped over the stones. "There must be another artery feeding into this one." He continued walking. "There it is."

She peered over his shoulder at the light. Another

tunnel appeared on the left, bringing more water in. "Which way do we go?"

"Straight. It's just a few houses ahead." He shone the light down the other branch. "They did a good job building this sewer."

She rolled her eyes. She would admire the engineering later. She just wanted to get out of here before she froze.

Rafe waded ahead, skimming his flashlight over the water to light the way. She started past the side tunnel, fighting the sudden increase in the water's force. But then a furry head swam past, bumping her knee.

A rat.

She shrieked and stumbled back, then lost her balance and fell. Icy water rushed to her neck. Panicked, terrified that the rat would get her, she scrabbled for purchase on the slippery stones. Rafe lunged back, grabbed her arm and hauled her to her feet.

"What happened?"

She instantly crowded against him, wanting to climb right into his skin. "A rat. Oh, God. It hit my knee." She shuddered and clutched his arm.

He trained the light on the oily stream. "I don't see anything."

"It was there. It came out from the side." Still clinging to him, she trembled hard.

He turned the light on her face. "Are you all right?"

Blinking, realizing that she was plastered against him and had a death grip on his arm, she forced herself to let go. "I'm fine. Except I stink," she added, still shivering, as his gaze traveled down her sodden clothes.

His eyes returned to hers. A sudden grin split his face, his white teeth flashing against his swarthy skin.

And he looked so startlingly handsome, so much like the man she'd fallen in love with that her heart contracted hard. And she couldn't help but smile back.

His dark eyes crinkled more, the amusement in them holding her fast. And she had the strongest urge to run her hands up his bristly jaw, plunge her fingers through his midnight-colored hair, and lose herself in his kiss.

That rogue thought shocked her, jolting her back to earth. Where had that impulse come from? She didn't behave like that anymore. And she had to forget the past, not start fantasizing about Rafe. Thoroughly off balance, she twisted the hem of her T-shirt and squeezed some water out.

"We're nearly there," Rafe said, the husky timbre of his voice accelerating her pulse. "Think you can manage?"

"I'm all right. Really." She glanced around the sewer, unable to meet his eyes. "Let's just hurry in case that rat had friends."

Rafe turned around with a nod and resumed hiking. Her teeth chattering, she trudged behind him, determined to get herself under control. She'd spent three years suppressing those feelings, and she wasn't about to let them best her now.

No matter how potent Rafe might be.

The water level gradually dropped, finally falling to ankle deep. A moment later, Rafe shifted the flashlight beam to the ceiling and stopped. "This should be it."

Shivering in her wet clothes, she glanced at the cement slab. "Where do you think it'll come out?"

"That's the million dollar question."

"And if it's near the guards?"

He slanted her a glance. "Then we run like hell."

He slid the backpack off his shoulder, took out a small, titanium crowbar, then handed her the pack. "There's a dry T-shirt in there if you want it."

"Oh, good." Grateful that he'd thought to bring it, she took the pack from his hands and set it on the stones near the wall. She stripped off her wet shirt and donned the dry one, then turned back to watch him work.

But Rafe hadn't moved. He stood immobile, his hot, dark gaze riveted on her torso, the naked heat in them sizzling clear to her toes. Her heart suddenly thundering, she tried to breathe.

His strong jaw flexed. His eyes turned even darker, as if he were fighting the hunger he felt. Then he turned without a word and started loosening the slab with a vengeance, the crowbar chinking against the stones.

Feeling thoroughly rattled, Gabi struggled to draw in a breath. Rafe obviously desired her. She could hardly miss the signs. But apparently he didn't *want* to want her. Which was fine. She didn't need the complication—even if his distance stung her pride.

Rafe inched the slab aside. Handing her the crowbar, he wiped his brow on his sleeve. "I'm going up to take a look. When I'm sure it's clear, I'll pull you through." He met her eyes, his expression carefully blank. "Unless you want to wait here for me to come back?"

Determined to keep her mind on their mission—and off the feelings threatening to shatter her self-control—she shook her head. "Not a chance." She needed to get her hands on that flash drive, no matter what.

"All right." His expression sobered. "But I'm serious, Gabi. If there's a problem, run back to the river. I'll catch up with you there."

"Be careful," she urged, suddenly tense.

He pushed the slab aside, the grating noise adding to her strained nerves. Then he positioned his hands around the opening and pulled himself upward, his biceps and shoulders bulging, the sinews standing out in his arms.

She'd always admired his strength. Back when they were teenagers, he'd followed a grueling physical workout—climbing ropes, scaling walls, doing hundreds of push-ups and pull ups daily—a regimen he'd obviously maintained.

His legs disappeared through the hole. A second later, his head reappeared. "Hand me the backpack," he whispered, and she lifted it to him.

He removed the pack, then stretched his arm back down. She clasped his hand, his work-roughened grip making her feel secure. She held her breath, his strength impressing her even more as he pulled her up.

She emerged into blazing sunshine. Blinking, she glanced around. They'd come out in an interior courtyard off one of the palace's wings. She swung her legs from the hole, then sprawled on the sun-warmed tiles while Rafe replaced the lid on the drain.

He motioned to a dense stand of bushes along one wall. She scrambled to her feet, grabbed the backpack and darted over, then ducked behind the shrubs. When he crawled in beside her, she released her pent-up breath.

For several minutes they didn't move. She peeked through the thick branches, her heart thudding fast, her shoulder crammed against Rafe's. She skipped her gaze from the fountain in the center of the patio to the ceramic pots brimming with flowers. Fuchsia bougainvilleas cascaded over the stucco walls.

Suddenly, she noticed puddles on the tiles around

the sewer. They'd left a trail of wet footprints leading straight to their hiding place in the shrubs. But before she could point it out, Rafe bent his dark head close. "I'm going inside," he said. "Wait here while I check things out."

"But—"

"Just until I'm sure it's safe. I'll be right back."

She closed her mouth, unable to argue. Rafe had more experience at this than she did. It made sense for him to scout ahead. She just prayed a guard didn't come by—and that those footprints evaporated first.

He rummaged in the backpack, took out a handful of lock-picking tools, and stuffed them into the back pocket of his jeans. Then he crawled from the bushes and sprinted across the patio to the French doors.

He tried the latch, but it didn't budge. He whipped out a pick and inserted it into the lock. A second later, the door opened, and he slipped inside.

Gabi peered between the branches, her pulse still racing, watching for signs of the guards. The fountain gurgled away. Sparrows landed on the rim, then took turns hopping into the water, fluttering their wings.

She fought back a rush of nerves, her anxiety growing despite the peaceful scene. Where was Rafe? What was he doing? Why hadn't he come back?

Then a movement across the patio caught her eye. A side door swung open, and a guard stepped out, an assault rifle looped over his chest. He turned and headed her way.

She stayed stock-still, her heart racketing around her rib cage. What if he saw the puddles she'd left—and found her crouching behind the shrubs?

The guard slowed as he reached the sewer. He

stopped, spun around, and everything inside her froze. He couldn't have missed those footprints. He had to know she was there. But then he continued walking across the patio and stopped outside the French doors.

Her mind raced. What was he doing? Why hadn't he sounded the alarm? Was he going to go after Rafe?

Her pulse hammered fast. The guard murmured into his radio, then glanced around the courtyard again. Gabi shrank back further into the bushes, certain he was going to shoot. But he strode back across the patio to the side door and disappeared.

Her breath whooshed out in a rush. She closed her eyes, the close call rattling her hard. But then she snapped them open again. It had to be a trick. The guard must have seen the puddles she'd left. He'd probably gone for backup—which meant she had to find Rafe and warn him fast.

Fearing the guard would return at any second, she scrambled out, darted to the French doors, and crept inside. Then she paused to let her eyes grow accustomed to the dim light. She'd entered a lavish bedroom suite, complete with museum-quality antiques, a plush oriental carpet, snores coming from the king-sized bed…

Her heart skittered hard. She fixed her gaze on the massive bed, unable to make out the figure beneath the sheets. She tore her gaze to the dress shoes beside the bed, the tuxedo draped over the nearby chair.

Ortiz.

Total panic consumed her. She shifted her weight from foot to foot, every survival instinct she possessed clamoring for her to flee. But she couldn't abandon Rafe. He was risking his life to find that flash drive. She couldn't save herself at his expense.

Terrified that Ortiz would hear her, she inched her way past the bed. She reached the door to the hallway and slowly cracked it open, her heart jackhammering so hard she was sure she'd wake Ortiz.

She peeked through the door at the empty corridor. Stumped, she racked her brain. Where was Rafe? Which way had he gone? She had to warn him about the guard.

The snoring stopped.

Horrified, she whirled around, her gaze slicing straight to the bed—into the eyes of the monster who'd destroyed her life.

Chapter 7

Ortiz's deranged eyes held her spellbound. And for one horrific moment she was back in her father's office, his blood splattered on the floor, the desk, the walls. Pain piercing her skull. Ortiz's huge hand squeezing her throat. Fighting, flailing, her world fading to black while sick excitement teemed in his eyes.

Terror rippled through her like a shock wave. The hair on her neck stood on end. She started trembling wildly, reliving the absolute vulnerability, the nightmarish loss of control she'd experienced at this monster's hands.

"Gabi!" Rafe's voice came from somewhere behind her. She struggled to move. *Run.* To pull herself out of this stupor and flee. But she couldn't breathe, couldn't think, couldn't tear her gaze from those evil eyes.

Ortiz swung to a sitting position, his expression triumphant, and grabbed the phone beside his bed—just as

Rafe reached through the doorway and yanked her arm. She stumbled backward into the hall, nearly sprawling on the marble floor, but Rafe managed to keep her upright as he dragged her along.

"What's wrong with you?" he growled. "Come on!"

She shook the fog from her stalled brain. He was right. What had happened to her back there? For three years she'd rehearsed for the moment when she would finally confront Ortiz—and instead of fighting back, she'd frozen, her mind flashing back to the violence, letting him seize the upper hand.

Rafe dropped her arm and ran. She sprinted behind him, disgusted at her reaction to Ortiz. They raced toward an open door at the end of the hallway, their footsteps pounding the marble tiles. But an armed guard materialized and blocked their way.

Gabi stumbled to a halt. The guard raised his weapon to fire. Rafe lunged sideways through an unlocked door, and she dove in after, panic threatening to overwhelm her. Somehow they had to escape.

She ran with Rafe through another bedroom. He shouldered open a door, and they burst onto another patio, this time behind the house.

"Over there," she gasped, spotting the stone wall at the back of the patio, a remnant of the medieval fortification that had once encircled the town. She raced toward its crumbling stone staircase, but Rafe beat her to it and leaped up the bottom step.

"Go!" he urged as he reached down and tugged her up.

Shouts rose from the patio behind them. She sprinted along the weed-choked staircase, her thigh muscles burning, as shots barked out from behind. Her pulse going berserk, she reached the top of the wide stone wall, and frantically glanced around.

Guards flooded into the courtyard behind them. She blanched at the twelve-foot drop to the ground, but couldn't see another way down.

"Jump!" Rafe said, echoing her thoughts. He grabbed her hand, taking her with him, and they sailed over the medieval wall.

She landed on the grass off balance, the impact wrenching her right ankle hard. Unable to halt her momentum, she tumbled forward, then sprawled facedown on the ground.

Rafe once again dragged her upright. "Hurry!" he said, but she didn't need his urging to know the guards were in pursuit. She sprinted toward the nearby trees, heedless of her throbbing ankle, more gunshots blasting her ears. Then she raced full out through the woods, crashing through the undergrowth and shrubs.

Her breath sawed. She leaped over logs and deadfall, pain stabbing her ankle with every step. But she gritted her teeth, refusing to slow her pace and further endanger Rafe. When they finally reached the river, they stopped.

She propped her hands on her knees, exhausted, her lungs fiery as she heaved in air. She blinked away the sweat stinging her eyes, her thighs quivering so hard she could barely stand.

"What happened?" Rafe asked.

Too breathless to speak, she shook her head.

"You're limping."

Her lungs still rasping, she straightened. "I…just… twisted my ankle. It's nothing. Really." She swiveled around and scanned the trees. "Which way should we go?"

"We need to split up."

"What? Why?"

"We'll never outrun them. It's the only way we can get away." A siren rose near the palace, underscoring his words.

She suffered a pang of guilt. He was right; they'd never outrun Ortiz—and it was all her fault. She'd left her hiding place in the bushes. She should have hurried to warn him. Instead she'd frozen around Ortiz, causing that deadly delay. And now her ankle was slowing them further, making it impossible to escape.

"Head to the Roman bridge," Rafe continued. "You know which one I mean?"

"Yes." It was a popular tourist spot at the edge of town, filled with restaurants and bars.

"I'll lead the police downstream, then circle back and meet you there."

"How will you get away?"

"Don't worry." His gaze narrowed on hers. "I mean it, Gabi. I know how to escape the police. Just meet me at the bridge."

She hesitated, grappling with conflicting emotions— fear that the guards would catch him, shame that she'd caused this disaster, guilt that Rafe was endangering his life to keep the guards from following her.

"Here. Take this." He fumbled in his pocket, then pressed something small and hard into her palm.

She opened her hand and blinked. *A flash drive.* She snapped her gaze to his. "Is this—?"

"I hope so. It was next to his laptop on his desk."

Relief billowed through her, so acute it nearly buckled her knees. *He'd found it.* And if this flash drive contained the proof she needed, she could convict Ortiz.

"Thank you," she choked out, hardly able to believe that she finally had the evidence in her hand.

But then another siren joined the first one. A helicopter flew over the palace, the deep reverberations of its rotors growing louder as it approached the woods.

"Hurry," Rafe said. "I'll meet you at the bridge. And Gabi…" His eyes held hers. "Don't do anything heroic. Just head to the bridge and wait."

Before she could answer, he sprinted away. She stuck the flash drive into her pocket, then started limping in the opposite direction, heading toward the outskirts of town. Seconds later, she glanced back, but Rafe had disappeared.

Alone now, she loped beside the river, running as fast as she could on her injured leg. But gunshots sounded in the distance, and she experienced a frisson of dread. Was Rafe all right? Had he managed to escape the guards? What would she do if they captured him?

For the last three years she'd done everything she could to protect him from Ortiz. She'd lied to him about that attack, certain he would try to avenge her if he knew the truth. She'd severed their relationship, intentionally making him hate her to ensure that he stayed away. And she'd suffered in lonely exile so Ortiz couldn't use him to get to her. And she'd never forgive herself if she caused Ortiz to harm him now.

But Rafe had grown up with professional thieves. He knew how to evade the police. Holding on to that hope—and trying to not imagine the worst-case scenario—she continued stumbling along the bank. The miles dragged by. Her ankle began to swell, throbbing so badly she could barely walk. Reduced to a hobble, she gritted her teeth and persevered, determined to make that rendezvous with Rafe.

After what seemed like an eternity, she finally caught sight of the bridge. Exhausted, she leaned against a pine tree to catch her breath and eyed the three stone arches that had spanned the river since Roman times. Now closed to vehicles, the bridge led to the medieval *puerta,* which had served as the town's main entrance when the fortified walls were intact. Across the river, restaurants, bars and souvenir shops had sprung up to service the tourists parking in the nearby lot.

She scanned the people walking across the bridge and posing for photos, the tourists sitting at the sidewalk cafés. But Rafe was nowhere in sight.

Barely able to stay upright, she limped toward a vacant bench near the riverbank. She snatched a newspaper from a nearby trash bin to use as cover, then collapsed on the bench to wait.

The river trickled by. Ducks waddled along the bank, hunting for crumbs. The clock in the *Plaza Mayor* struck two, and the anxiety humming inside her swelled to a roar. What was taking Rafe so long? Had he been captured? Hurt? And what if he *had* been arrested? What would he want her to do?

Trying to distract herself, she pulled the flash drive from her pocket and turned it over, studying the key-shaped logo on the metal sides. It looked so harmless, so ordinary—yet held information Ortiz was willing to kill for, secrets vital to the security of País Vell.

A sudden thought snaked through her mind. She didn't have to wait for Rafe. If this flash drive contained what she expected, she had everything she needed to incriminate Ortiz. She could contact the prime minister and arrange to deliver the flash drive to a secure location, just as she'd originally planned.

Rafe probably wouldn't mind. He'd never really required her help. And he already had the ring he needed to secure his father's release.

Better yet, if she left now, she could keep her secrets about the past intact—protecting them both.

She shifted her gaze to the restaurant and spotted a pay phone, but her conscience instantly rebelled. She couldn't do it. No matter how tempting, she couldn't go back on her word to Rafe. He already believed she'd betrayed him once—and no way could she do it twice.

Especially when he was out there right now for her sake, risking his life.

But neither could she sit here, wasting time. Growing antsy, she scanned the café tables crowded with tourists, the souvenir T-shirts hanging from racks. Then a sign in the restaurant window advertising free internet access caught her eye.

Her pulse sped up. Should she risk it? These tourists probably hadn't heard the latest news. No one had paid her any attention so far. And before she delivered the flash drive to the prime minister, she should make sure she had the right one. She could pop into the restaurant, take a peek at the flash drive's contents, and hurry back out. Rafe would never even know she'd gone.

She flipped that over in her mind, weighing the dangers, but the memory of her father's face in that newscast firmed her resolve. She had to bring down his murderer, no matter what the risk. Determined, she rose and limped up the bank toward the restaurant, then threaded her way through the café tables to the open door.

Once inside the restaurant, she looked around, spotting the computers in the back near the kitchen door. Keeping her head down, she headed to the rear of the restaurant, found a vacant machine and sat.

She eased out her breath in relief. *So far so good.* Now she just had to view the flash drive and get out.

She inserted the drive in the USB port, then went to the computer's file management system to open it. But the old machine was sluggish, testing her patience, and she drummed her hand on the desk. While she waited, she scanned the busy room, noting the young family at a nearby table, the teenaged boy at the computer beside her, a group of backpackers studying maps by the door.

The teenager glanced her way. She quickly averted her face, hoping he wouldn't recognize her without Rafe. But with that huge reward Ortiz had posted for their capture…

Silently urging the computer to hurry, she double clicked on the icon for the drive. A second later, the screen changed to silver—and a log-in prompt appeared.

Her stomach fell. Of course the flash drive was password encrypted. What had she expected? The Americans wouldn't have passed along intelligence of this magnitude without putting precautions in place.

Frowning, she studied the screen, and realized it was worse than that. Not only was it password encrypted, but there was a warning on the screen that she would only be allowed ten tries. After ten invalid attempts to enter the password, the contents would self-destruct.

Racking her brain for options, she slumped back in

her wooden chair. The diplomat must have brought the password with him. He'd probably carried it separately from the flash drive in case of theft. And it could be anything—a computer-generated sequence, random letters and numbers, a formerly agreed-upon word…

Or the inscription on that ancient ring?

Her excitement rose. Could the password possibly be that simple? It would explain Ortiz's interest in the ring. She leaned forward, knowing it was worth a shot.

She typed in the Latin motto—*Morior invictus*—and paused. The password was probably case-sensitive. She backspaced, capitalized the *I,* then hesitated again. What about the spaces? Should she run the words together or leave them as is? She didn't want to waste attempts.

The teenager beside her stood, and she scooted over to give him room to pass. He walked across the room and spoke to a waiter, and the two men looked her way.

They'd recognized her. She ducked her head and swore. She had to hurry and leave before they called the police. But she couldn't go yet. She needed to make sure she had the proof.

Suddenly feeling frantic, she swung her attention back to the monitor—but the screen began to flicker, and a bar appeared, like files loading at breakneck speed. Only the files weren't loading; they were deleting!

She stared at it, aghast. This shouldn't be happening. She hadn't entered a password yet. How could she have triggered a command to destroy the files?

Horrified, she grabbed the flash drive and jerked it out of the machine—too late. What ever that drive had contained, she'd just wiped it clean.

* * *

Rafe parked the stolen scooter in the lot beside the restaurant and headed toward the Roman bridge. For the past hour he'd led the police on a convoluted chase through town—running through alleys and side streets, leaving evidence to lead them astray. He'd finally ditched them on the other side of town, using the scooter to get away. But he didn't have much time. He had to find Gabi and get her to safety before Ortiz's men tracked them down.

He neared the bridge and slowed, then scanned the milling crowd. Tourists strolled along the banks of the river. More people stood on the bridge, snapping photos of the medieval town. A tour bus started up nearby, and several last-minute stragglers scurried to climb aboard.

Rafe stopped and crossed his arms, a bad feeling seeping through his gut. She'd had plenty of time. She should have been here by now. Unless she'd lied...

Not wanting to believe it, he surveyed the crowd again. But he couldn't ignore the fact that she wasn't there.

His pessimism growing, he walked down the bank to the river, scooped up a small, flat stone, and skipped it to the other side. He never should have trusted her. Why he had, he couldn't say. He *knew* she was a good actress. Hell, the first time he'd laid eyes on her, when he was just nineteen, she'd been performing in a community play.

He made a sound of disgust. That woman had bewitched him from the start. Enchanted by her beauty, he'd followed her to a bar that night—and forever changed his life. He'd gone straight because of her. He'd broken with his family to become the kind of man she deserved. He'd ignored reality, overlooking the aristo-cratic chasm between them, believing that love would be enough.

Love. He snorted at his lunacy. While he'd offered her his heart, she'd strung him along, promising to love him forever, then dumping him without a qualm.

It appeared she hadn't changed.

He released a hiss. He was a fool, all right. He had a weak spot around that woman—and apparently always would.

A pair of swans floated by. A couple trudged past, cameras slung around their necks. And he knew there was no point hanging around. Gabi wasn't going to mag-ically appear. He had to put her out of his mind, take the diplomat's ring to Ortiz and bargain for his father's release. In hindsight, he never should have given her that flash drive, but he would have to make do.

Still seething, he climbed the bank and headed toward the parking lot where he'd left the bike. But then a police car screeched to a stop in front of the res-taurant, catching his eye. Several royal guards jumped out, their weapons drawn.

He froze. They must have seen him—unless Gabi had tipped them off.... But no, even she wouldn't be that cruel. They must have followed him here.

He glanced at the road and bridge, calculating the safest route out. But then another car drove up. More guards piled out, converging on the restaurant. Tourists stopped and stared.

Rafe frowned, taken aback. The guards weren't look-ing his way. Then what...

He turned his gaze to the restaurant and spotted the internet sign. A stark chill robbed him of breath.

She wouldn't. She would. Oh, hell.

Dread tumbling through him, he took off for the restaurant at a run. He'd bet his life Gabi had gone inside.

And unless he could pull off a miracle, she was about to die.

Chapter 8

Rafe leaped aboard the scooter, then sped down the alley behind the restaurant, racing full-out to beat the guards. They were fanning out, taking up positions on the surrounding roads and buildings, only seconds from barging inside.

But had Gabi noticed the danger in time?

His pulse rocketed as he roared toward the restaurant. He swerved around a Dumpster, nearly colliding with a man carting trash.

"Hey!" the man yelled. "Watch out!"

But Rafe didn't dare slow. He zoomed to the service bay and slammed on his brakes, just as the door crashed open and Gabi came flying out.

Her terrified eyes connected with his. She jumped down the steps, wobbling on her injured ankle, and lunged the remaining distance to his side.

"Hurry," he urged as she grabbed his shoulder for bal-

ance and swung her leg over the seat. He rammed the
bike into gear and gunned the engine, nearly upending
them both. Then he twisted back hard on the throttle
and raced down the alley toward the road.

Adrenaline coursed through him. They only had seconds to escape those guards. He sped full-bore toward
the end of the alley, checking in his side mirror to make
sure no one was behind.

"Hold on!" he warned, and Gabi tightened her grip
on his waist. He hit the brakes, made a sharp right turn
into a footpath barely wide enough to accommodate the
bike. Then he cranked the throttle and tore down the
narrow path, nearly scraping the buildings' stone sides.
When they reached the next alley over, he started zig-
zagging through a warren of back streets at the edge of
town.

"Where are we going?" Gabi asked, her voice close
to his ear.

"To a trail I know." They couldn't take the main road
out of town. Ortiz would have every exit blocked. Rafe
angled down another cobblestone street, spotted the
wrought-iron lamp post he used as a landmark, and
veered onto a dirt trail obscured by brush. The bike
bumped and jostled on the uneven ground.

For several minutes they didn't speak. Rafe concen-
trated on maneuvering through the rough terrain, for
once thankful for his family of thieves. His grandfather
had shown him the ancient smuggling routes through
the mountains—routes he doubted the police could find.

They reached the river a few minutes later, and he
followed it upstream. When he spotted a wooden foot-
bridge, he brought the bike to a stop.

Trying to catch his breath, he eyed the bridge. The

river gurgled past, sparkling through the gaps in the rotting boards. "We'd better walk across," he said.

Gabi climbed off the bike, her gaze on the weathered bridge. "Can you get the scooter across?"

"I hope so." They didn't have time to cross the mountains on foot.

Gabi led the way. Rafe pushed the bike behind her, her pronounced limp making him scowl. She'd had no business risking her life back there. Those guards would have shot her on sight. But that discussion would have to wait. They had to distance themselves from the village first.

Trying to keep his mind off Gabi—and the stark fear still threatening to overwhelm him when he thought of that close call—he hurried across the bridge. Then they hopped back on the scooter and continued along the trail. Not long after, they reached the old cement road that had connected the mountain hamlets before the modern highway was built. Rafe turned onto the one-lane road and opened the scooter's throttle, heading deeper into the hills.

The miles whizzed by. Rafe took the bike to its limit, its quiet buzz filling the air. The afternoon sun climbed high in the sky.

But then the rumble of a helicopter reached his ears. Gabi's hands clutched his waist. "Rafe—"

"I hear it." His heart suddenly thudding, he veered off the winding road toward a copse of pines. He hit the brakes, and they both leaped off and ran toward the cover of trees. He shoved the scooter into a thicket of brambles, then lunged into some bushes behind Gabi and hunkered beside her to wait.

The deep reverberations grew louder. The ground

vibrated beneath his feet as the chopper steadily approached. Rafe glued his gaze on the strip of sky barely visible between the trees, the pungent scent of pine needles filling his lungs.

The branches above them began to thrash. The deafening noise drew closer, rattling his teeth. Then the chopper appeared overhead, and he stilled at the sinister sight. *A military gunship.* Exactly what was on that flash drive that Ortiz would go to this extent?

The chopper moved slowly past, the ominous drum of its rotors fading away. But the turmoil inside Rafe grew stronger, the enormity of their predicament hitting him hard. Ortiz had worldwide resources to call on—air power, troops, an arsenal containing weapons of every sort. How could they hope to fight that?

Grim now, he crawled from the bushes, then reached back to help Gabi out. But the silkiness of her skin, the vulnerable feel of her soft hand made something inside him snap. Bad enough they had Ortiz to fight without constantly tipping him off.

"What *the hell* were you doing back there?" he demanded.

Her lips turned flat. She brushed the twigs from her shirt and jeans, then deliberately crossed her arms. "I was trying to get a look at the flash drive. I wanted to see what was on it."

"By nearly getting us killed? I told you to wait for me at the bridge."

"I did wait. For a long time. But when you didn't show up—"

"I was leading the guards away, making sure we could get out of town without the police force catching up."

Her cheeks flushed. "I know. It's just…I saw the internet sign, and I thought we might not be near a computer again. And I wanted to make sure we had the right thing before we risked calling the prime minister."

So she'd risked her life instead. He worked his jaw, his blood turning cold at the thought of Gabi around Ortiz. "So what was on it?"

She fiddled with the hem of her shirt. "I don't know."

"You didn't see it?"

"Not exactly." Guilt crept into her eyes. "I put the flash drive in the computer and…something happened."

He went dead still, her evasiveness putting him on alert. "What do you mean *something happened?*"

"A prompt came on the screen, telling me I had to enter a password, so I decided to try the inscription, the one on the ring, *Morior invictus.* I typed it in, but I wasn't sure if I should leave a space or not. So I sat there for a second, trying to decide. And then suddenly, the screen flickered and erased the files."

His heart missed a beat. He gave his head a hard shake, certain he'd heard her wrong.

But she shot him a look of chagrin. "I tried to remove the flash drive, but I couldn't get it out in time. And the files just…disappeared."

He stared at her for several heartbeats, feeling numb. They'd almost died escaping the castle. They'd broken into Ortiz's palace and had nearly been shot. And now they had the guards closing in, military gunships hunting them down—and all for nothing. The information was gone.

Still unable to believe it, he turned on his heels and walked to the edge of the field. Then he stared out at the broken corn stalks, trying to wrap his mind around the news. At least with that flash drive they'd had some leverage, a chance to defeat Ortiz. But now...

He turned to face her again. "You're sure the files are gone?"

"I think so. Maybe a computer expert could retrieve them, but I don't know."

He plunged his hand through his hair. Now what were they going to do? They couldn't stay on the defensive, but they had nothing to use to fight back. "You should have waited for me."

"Why? Do you know something about computers?"

"No, but at least I could have made sure we got away before anyone spotted us."

Her shoulders hunched. "I thought I'd be fine. No one was paying any attention to me. And I didn't think it would take long to check the files."

"You didn't think, period. Christ, Gabi. You saw that helicopter. Don't you realize what we're up against?"

Her chin came up. "I know *exactly* what we're up against."

"Then how could you take such a bloody risk?"

Her eyes blazed. "Because Ortiz murdered my father. I'll do anything it takes to get that man behind bars."

"You don't know that he killed him. You're guessing. And what if you're wrong? What if you're risking your life and he wasn't even to blame?"

"I'm not wrong. He's the murderer."

"How could you know that? You weren't there when he got killed."

Her startled eyes connected with his. The color leached from her face. And suddenly, the truth slammed through him, robbing him of breath. *"You were there?"*

She whirled around and gave him her back. Dread

pounding through him, he stalked around to face her, unwilling to believe what he'd seen in her eyes. "What happened?" he demanded.

She averted her eyes. "I—"

"The *truth*, Gabi. Damn it, you owe me that. I'm in this as much as you are."

Her gaze returned to his, the desolation in her eyes sinking his heart. "Yes," she whispered, her voice broken. "I was there."

Incredulous, he stared at her. She'd seen Ortiz murder her father. Nothing could have shocked him more.

For an eternity, he couldn't speak. He could only gape, dumbfounded at the woman he'd loved—the woman it seemed he never knew.

Then the sound of a tractor penetrated his awareness. He shook himself back to the present, but his world felt oddly adrift. "We have to go," he said. They needed shelter, a place where they wouldn't be so exposed. "But we'll talk about this later."

He'd make damned sure of that.

They rode through the mountains for miles, passing time-forgotten hamlets, following tractor trails and hiking paths as they searched for a safe place to hide. Gabi clung to Rafe's waist on the back of the scooter, exhausted, her eyes stinging from the constant wind. But she would have gladly endured the misery of the bike forever to avoid the confrontation ahead.

They puttered through another *aldea*, not far from her family's ancestral estate, and she let out a weary sigh. She owed Rafe an explanation; she couldn't argue that. But did she dare tell him the truth?

The thought terrified her. She'd held it inside for

so many years, never telling another soul except the counselor she'd seen in Spain. But she couldn't seem to lie around Rafe. And frankly, she *wanted* to tell him the truth. She longed to open up and confide in him, to stop pretending, stop acting, stop hiding the facts of that dreadful night.

They came out of a hairpin curve, and Rafe reclined in his seat, his muscled back brushing her chest. And a desperate yearning swept through her, the desire to wrap her arms around him, rest her cheek on those massive shoulders, and take solace in his strength and warmth, indulging in the comfort she'd denied herself for years.

And really, what option did she have? She could abort her mission and leave Rafe in an attempt to conceal her secret—but for how long? They couldn't hide forever. Ortiz would eventually capture them both.

So what harm could the truth do now? Ortiz was already intending to kill them. Telling Rafe about that night wouldn't make anything worse.

Except for her.

They zipped past a familiar landmark, a twelfth-century Knights Templar church her father had once taken her to see, and she struggled to conquer the fear.

Ortiz had altered the course of her life that night. And during the ensuing years she'd drawn inward, trying to deal with the pain and loss. She'd convinced herself that she hadn't hurt Rafe that badly, that he'd found someone else to love by now, and that without her, his life had moved on.

But she couldn't fool herself anymore. Since returning to País Vell, she'd witnessed his resentment, his anger, the bitterness he still harbored after all this time. So maybe she owed him this. Maybe it was time to expose the truth of that dreadful night and give him the peace he deserved.

No matter the cost to her.

A few miles later, Rafe pulled into a long dirt driveway leading to a tiny farmhouse nearly obscured by the overgrown shrubs. She scanned the abandoned hay fields surrounding the house, the weeds crowding the rutted drive, the antigovernment slogans spray painted on the exposed patches of wall. And she realized with a start that they'd crossed the border into the former Reino Antiguo, the separatist region of the country where even the royal guards refused to go.

Rafe circled the house and cut the engine. She climbed off the scooter, her ankle hurting like the devil, wanting desperately to forget her upcoming confession, and crawl into a bed and sleep. But she'd deceived Rafe long enough.

"You think it's safe to stay here?" she asked, glancing around. The separatists didn't take to outsiders, especially those from País Vell.

"It's more dangerous not to right now. We'll never make it into France or Spain unless we go on foot. They'll have all the old border crossings blocked. And even if we did get across, it wouldn't do any good with our faces all over the news."

He was right. She'd heard that newscast. And while the separatists might not like them, they were also less likely to cooperate with the authorities—unless they wanted that reward.

Rafe dismounted and stretched his back. While he parked the scooter behind some shrubs, Gabi hobbled inside the farmhouse and glanced around the dim room. The untrimmed shrubs blocked the broken windows. More slogans covered the peeling plaster walls. She eyed the cracked cement floor, the rickety table and chairs, the ancient wood-burning stove. But the house didn't really matter. The moment of reckoning had come.

Rafe came inside a second later. Then he stopped, crossed his muscled arms over his chest, and leveled his gaze on her. "All right. Let's hear it."

She'd thought she'd prepared herself, that she could relate the story calmly, dispassionately, as if it had happened to someone else. But a sweat broke out on her spine. Her heart began to sprint. Feeling far too vulnerable under Rafe's scrutiny, she crossed the room to a window and stared through the shattered glass.

"It was a Friday night," she began. "About eight o'clock." Her voice wobbled, and she cleared her throat. "I'd finished work about five, but I remembered something I had to do, so I went back to the office. I didn't want to leave it until after the weekend."

Truth be told, she'd been trying hard to impress her father in the year since she'd returned from studying abroad. She'd wanted to prove that she was dependable, levelheaded, that he could trust her to make the right decisions about the business she would inherit someday *and* her personal life—including marrying Rafe.

"And?" Rafe prompted from behind her.

"And I was in a hurry so I took the elevator. I got to my father's office, and the door was open. That surprised me because I thought he'd already left. He'd told me that he had a business dinner at our country estate that night."

She inhaled, her breath suddenly ragged, as if she'd just run twenty miles. *But she had to tell him the truth.*

"I went in…and I knew right away something was wrong. I felt…danger. I should have left."

"Why didn't you?"

She shook her head. She'd asked herself that question a thousand times. "I don't know. I just…froze. It seemed unreal, as if it were happening to someone else, like I was in a dream. And then I heard a noise—a grunt, then a thump. Like a body falling to the floor. I thought my father was sick or having a heart attack, so I raced inside.

"He…" Her voice quivered. She stared unseeing at the broken glass, trapped in the hellish memories, trying not to remember the stench, the blood, the fear. "He was dead. Beaten. Badly. The killer was still there. He was wearing a black hood. He turned toward me, and I could see his eyes…." Those horrifying, deranged eyes. "I tried…I tried to get away."

Her entire body shook. Nausea swamped her belly, a cold sweat drenching her skin.

"I tried to run," she whispered. "But he…he caught me. Choked me."

"Gabi…" Rafe's voice was raw.

"No. Wait. There's more." She had to tell him now or she never would. "He raped me." She shuddered and closed her eyes, reliving the shock, the pain, the crazed excitement she'd seen in his eyes. "He kept squeezing my throat, then waiting, giving me just enough air to survive."

To make the horror last.

She gasped for breath. Trembling, her legs threatening to buckle, she forced herself to face Rafe. He looked poleaxed, shocked, his handsome face sheet white.

"He thought I was dead, but I…I recognized his

voice. That laugh." That sick, triumphant laugh. "He left, and I crawled to the stairwell and sat there for awhile." Terrified, bleeding, and in shock.

"Finally, I heard a siren. I knew he was coming back, and that his men would cover for him. Or they'd think *I'd* murdered my father. There was so much blood on my clothes..."

She pressed her shaking hand to her lips, not wanting to remember the sight. "I made it home." It had been the longest drive of her life. Then she'd huddled in her apartment, feeling powerless, numb, betrayed.

"Oh, God, Gabi..."

"I did all the wrong things. I showered. I threw away my clothes. I knew no one would believe me. How could I fight the head of the police?" Hysteria tinged her voice. "I even blamed myself, thinking I should have fought harder, that if I'd only gotten there sooner..."

She'd even wondered if her adventurous, risk-taking nature had somehow contributed to the attack—which she now knew was absurd. But at the time...

"Why didn't you call me?" His voice came out rough.

"I couldn't think at first. I felt...dirty, disgusted." Demeaned. "I couldn't face anyone." Especially Rafe.

"I would have helped you."

Her stomach wrenched. "I know that." He would have raced to her rescue and avenged her with his dying breath. That soul-deep honor spoke to the core of who he was, the reason he'd transformed his life.

"But I also knew you'd go after Ortiz. And I saw what he did to my father. I couldn't let him kill you, too."

Rafe's eyes turned deadly. He let out a savage sound. "I would have killed him first."

"And then what? Spent the rest of your life behind

bars? There was no way I could let you destroy your life." Bad enough that Ortiz had shattered hers.

"So you broke off our engagement."

"I was afraid he'd use you to get to me, and I wanted to keep you safe." So she'd severed their relationship in the cruelest way she knew how.

At first she'd refused his calls, hoping her silence would drive him away. But when he'd persevered and shown up at her apartment two days after her father's death, she'd hurled those hurtful words at him, making sure she destroyed his love.

Rafe turned on his heel, walked across the room to another window, then braced his forearm on the wall and stared out.

"After the funeral, I left País Vell," she continued. She couldn't bear to see Rafe, and couldn't chance running into Ortiz. "I moved to Spain, and I… I was pretty depressed for a while." Suffering from nightmares, lost in a reclusive tailspin, drinking herself senseless to cope.

"I finally got counseling. It helped." She'd learned to stop blaming herself for the rape, to grieve for her murdered father and the loss of the man she loved.

And she'd channeled her anger and shame into one all-consuming goal. *Revenge.*

"Ortiz reported the murder as a robbery gone bad," she continued. "When I didn't contradict him, he probably thought I hadn't recognized him." And that like so many other rape victims, she'd been too traumatized to report the truth.

"I moved my corporate headquarters to Spain and took over my father's business. Then I tried to figure out what got him killed. That's when I discovered the spy group and his secret life."

She eased out a shaky breath, the worst of the story done. "I assumed he'd come across something that incriminated Ortiz. But Ortiz is clever. It's taken me all this time to find a clue. And when I saw the diplomat's message, I knew that was it, the proof I'd been waiting for all this time."

The proof she'd just erased.

Her heart plummeted, the irony of the mess she'd made finally sinking in. She wasn't only back to square one. By returning to País Vell, she'd done exactly what she'd spent the last three years trying to avoid.

She'd brought the danger to Rafe.

Rafe stared through the cobwebs covering the window, the bombshell Gabi had dropped detonating his world. Everything he'd believed—about Gabi, the past, that night—was wrong.

Dazed, he shook his head, struggling to reconcile her version of events with his own. But she'd told him the truth. He had no doubts about that—which meant *he* was squarely to blame.

He hung his head, unable to believe how badly he'd screwed up. He should have been there that night to protect her. He should have seen through her desperate lies. And he should have hunted down Ortiz, not resting until he'd made that bastard pay for his crimes.

Instead, he'd turned on Gabi. He'd blamed her, resented her, vilified her—when she'd suffered through hell to keep him safe.

He exhaled, unable to believe the fool he'd been. He'd totally failed her. How could he ever make amends?

He would kill Ortiz. That was a given. That scumbag was as good as dead.

But Gabi... He turned around to face her. Her beautiful eyes searched his, her vulnerability a sucker punch to his heart. "Gabi," he said helplessly. How could he apologize for what he'd done?

He walked to where she stood. Then he lifted his trembling hand and cradled her cheek, tracing her silken jaw with his thumb. "I'm sorry," he said, knowing the words were inadequate, that nothing could erase the pain she'd endured.

"I'm sorry, too," she whispered. "I had to drive you away. But I never meant what I said. Any of it. It was all lies. I just...wanted you to know."

He pulled her into his arms. She stood unyielding for a moment, her slender frame stiff against his. Then she slid her arms around his waist, and sagged against his chest. He rested his cheek on her satin hair and closed his eyes.

For long moments he just stood there, his throat choked tight, holding the woman he'd loved in his arms. Unable to imagine the horror she'd endured. Wishing he could magically undo the past. Knowing he'd abandoned her when she'd needed him most.

And that he'd never forgive himself for that.

Several heartbeats later, she straightened and stepped away. He dropped his hands, giving her the distance she needed, but regrets still swarmed inside.

He couldn't change the past. He couldn't regain the love they'd lost, or atone for his lack of faith. All he could do was destroy Ortiz.

But his father would pay the price.

Chapter 9

Caught between conflicting choices, Rafe watched Gabi hobble to the wooden table and tried to decide what to do. He had to take down Ortiz; he had no doubts about that. He owed it to Gabi to avenge that vicious attack.

But how could he abandon his father? How could he renege on his solemn vow? How could he maintain his self-respect—and find the redemption he'd sought for years—if he let the dying man down?

A dull ache formed behind his eyebrows. He exhaled, knowing there had to be a solution, some way to accomplish both goals. But what it was, he didn't know.

His stomach rumbled in the silence. Realizing they hadn't eaten in hours, he reluctantly turned his attention to their more immediate problem—surviving the night.

"We need food," he said. Along with gas for the

scooter and bedding so they could sleep. "I'll head back to that last village we went through and see what I can find."

"I'll go with you." Gabi struggled to rise from her chair.

"No, you stay here. You need to stay off that foot." He crossed the room to her side. "How bad is it?" They'd been so busy escaping the royal guards that he hadn't had time to check.

"Not bad. It's just sore."

"Let me see." He dropped to one knee, carefully cradled her foot in his hands, and pushed up the hem of her jeans. Her slender ankle had swollen, her skin turned warm to the touch. He unlaced her sneaker and peeled it off.

"Does this hurt?" He gently rotated the joint.

She winced. "A little."

He studied the stress lines bracketing her mouth and frowned. "It's probably sprained. Keep it elevated while I'm gone. I'll get some ice in town. An Ace bandage, too, if I can find one."

She opened her mouth to argue, but he cut her off. "Gabi… Can you just listen to me for once and stay here?"

"But there's no need. My ankle can wait for another hour. And I can blend in better than you can."

"Not in a village that small. Any stranger's going to stick out."

"At least I speak the dialect. I grew up near here, remember?"

"Yeah, I remember." He could hardly forget her family's medieval fortress or the garden where he'd proposed. "But you still need to rest your ankle. We might have to hike later on." And given the dark circles bruising her eyes, she'd collapse if she didn't sleep soon.

"I guess that makes sense." Reluctance tugged at her voice. "But be careful. And try not to talk to anyone."

His mouth slid into a grin. "Just keep my mouth shut, right?"

"Just come back."

His gaze connected with hers, the hint of vulnerability in her golden eyes making something unravel around his heart. "Don't worry. I will." No matter what else happened, he wouldn't let her down again.

"I'm counting on that," she whispered.

A warm feeling seeped through his chest. And for a moment, time slid away, and he was back with the woman he'd loved. He took in the gentle slope of her cheeks, the curve of her graceful neck, the lilting swell of her lips. Damn, but he'd worshipped this woman. She'd been his perfect mate—erotic, exciting, smart.

But he'd fallen for more than that. He'd loved her generous heart, her unpretentious ways, the fact that she'd wanted *him,* that she'd seen beyond the surface to the man he was, the honorable man he could become.

The man she inspired him to be.

And suddenly, he couldn't avoid the question he'd been trying to ignore. Gabi had admired him, approved of him, loved him. He'd known that deep in his heart. So why had he believed her lies?

Not sure he would like the answer, he rose and left the farmhouse, then set out for the village on the bike. In hindsight, her deception never should have taken him in. Her abrupt decision to dump him, her sudden scorn for what he'd achieved, her uncharacteristic declaration that she'd only marry a man from her social class had all been glaring clues.

So why had he ignored the truth? Why had he preferred to believe the worst of her instead of seeing through her blatant lies?

He turned onto the paved road, cranked the throttle, then took the scooter to the limit, racing toward the hamlet nestled against the steep hills. But he couldn't outrun the answer, no matter how hard he pushed the bike. He and Gabi had grown up in different worlds. He'd come from a family of thieves. She'd descended from the aristocracy, a world of tradition and prestige; while he'd lived in a shabby apartment, her family owned an ancestral estate, complete with porticoes and marble floors. Still, traditions had never impressed him. And he'd never felt impoverished, not with the high-priced jewels that passed through his family's hands. But no matter how thrilling the game his family had played, no matter the satisfaction he'd felt puzzling through security systems and outwitting the police, he'd lacked the one thing Gabi had had from birth—respect.

Meeting Gabi had driven that chasm home. And from that moment on, he'd had one goal, to earn the respect he'd never had—from Gabi, from society, from himself.

Her rejection had flayed his pride. It seemed that nothing he'd done—going straight, earning his college degree, founding a lucrative business that could support her in the style she deserved—had convinced her of his worth.

Or so he'd told himself.

The question was *why*.

He frowned, wishing he could sidestep the answer, but he couldn't avoid the truth. Because beneath that injured pride lay something else, something far more powerful, the gut-deep fear that she'd been right.

He took the bike to the limit, racing into the cooling wind. He'd been scared, all right, scared that he didn't deserve her, that he wasn't worthy of respect. And rather than face that fear, he'd withdrawn in bitter outrage, blaming her for rejecting him.

His mouth crooked up at the irony. She *had* been right. He hadn't deserved her, but not for the reasons he'd supposed, but because he'd failed her when she'd needed him most.

The village church came into view. Rafe downshifted to slow the scooter as the asphalt gave way to stones. He'd acted like a bloody coward, abandoning Gabi in her hour of need. So how did he fix that now? He could start by avenging her rape. No matter what else happened, Ortiz had to pay for his crimes. But Rafe had also promised to free his father, and he couldn't go back on his word.

Unable to solve that dilemma, he released a heavy sigh. Then he turned his mind to an easier problem, finding supplies. He puttered past a church and bakery, a bar with pro-separatist slogans spray painted on the sides.

Recalling Gabi's advice, he bypassed the stores and turned onto a narrow dirt road heading farther into the hills. He eyed a farmhouse at the edge of town, but a barking dog spurred him on. He rounded a bend, neared a ramshackle house with threadbare sheets hanging on the line, and braked again. *No dog.* Encouraged, he scanned the barn and machinery shed, then spotted the farmers across the field, their tractor clattering as they baled their hay.

His conscience twinged. He hated to cause these people grief when they obviously worked hard for the little they had. But he didn't see many options with Ortiz closing in fast.

He parked beside the machinery shed, found a gas can on a dusty shelf inside, and filled up the scooter's tank. That done, he walked around the garden to the back of the house and strolled through the unlocked door.

Working quickly, he scavenged two blankets from a bedroom cupboard, along with a couple throw pillows from a nearby chair. Then he went into the kitchen in search of food. He gathered some leftover bread and cheese, a bottle of homemade wine, and two clay yogurt containers that would serve as little cups. Another quick circuit yielded a first aid kit, which he added to the pile. He rolled everything into a blanket and slung it over his back, hobo-style.

Then he paused. He had to leave some money, but where? He couldn't put it any place visible. He wanted them to find it eventually, but not soon enough to alert the police.

Thinking hard, he scanned the canisters lined up on the counter, the dishes drying beside the sink. Then his gaze stalled on a pair of rubber boots by the door. He strode over, picked up one of the boots and stuffed several bills inside. Setting the boot back down next to a pile of newspapers, he turned to go. But a photograph on the front page of the newspaper caught his eye, and he froze.

A deep sense of foreboding gathered inside him. His father had made the headlines. That couldn't mean anything good.

His heart thudding, he picked up the paper and skimmed the news. His father had tried to escape from prison. The guards had caught him and opened fire. He'd survived the gunshots—barely—but the prognosis wasn't good.

Rafe crumpled the paper, a hot rush of anger scorching his gut. The story was bogus. His father never would have tried to flee. He was too damned weak from the cancer to get out of bed, let alone sprint across the prison yard and climb a fence.

This had nothing to do with his father, nothing to do with any supposed "escape." This cold-blooded shooting was a warning, clear and simple, a message from Ortiz to Rafe.

If he didn't surrender immediately, his father would forfeit his life.

Gabi took one look at Rafe as he strode into the abandoned farmhouse and knew instantly that something was wrong. Ignoring her tender ankle, she leaped to her feet. "What happened? Did someone see you? Do we need to leave?"

"No, it's not that." He stalked across the room to the table, his eyes furious, a bundle slung over his shoulder. "It's my father." He set the sack on the table, unknotted the top, and handed her the newspaper he'd stuck inside.

A photo of an older man resembling Rafe covered the front page. *Oh, no.* "He didn't—"

"Not yet." He grabbed a bottle of wine from the pile and began removing the cork.

But the news had to be bad. Her pulse quickening, she skimmed the article beneath the photo, her horror mounting with every word. "You don't really think he tried to escape?"

Rafe raised a sardonic brow. "Hardly. The last time I saw him he could barely lift his head."

"So Ortiz did this." That fit. Torturing a dying man was exactly his style. And Rafe knew that. Knowing how helpless he must feel, she sighed. "Do you think he's trying to force you to turn yourself in?"

"That's my guess." Rafe pulled out the cork from the bottle with a muffled pop and filled two empty ceramic yogurt cups with wine. He downed his in a single gulp.

"So what do you want to do?" she asked as he splashed more wine into his cup.

He grimaced. "What can we do?"

She sank into her chair. "We don't have much choice. We have to turn over the ring."

He shot her a look of disbelief. "And then what? What about convicting Ortiz?"

Her throat went tight. She picked up her cup and sipped her wine. For the past three years she'd plotted revenge. She'd lived it, breathed it, longed for it with every fiber of her being. It had given meaning to her shattered life, providing her with a reason to live. Nothing mattered more than avenging her father's death.

But if it meant denying Rafe's father his chance for freedom, was it worth the cost?

She lifted her gaze to Rafe, the bleakness in his midnight-colored eyes twisting her heart. And she knew right then that she couldn't do it. She'd already hurt him enough.

Her heavy sigh broke the silence in the room. "I never thought I'd say this, but maybe we should forget about Ortiz. Maybe the past doesn't matter now."

"It matters." Rafe's voice came out flat.

"Not necessarily."

Rafe hooked a chair with his foot and sat. "How can you say that? He raped you. He killed your father, and he's damned well going to pay."

"Listen, Rafe. I want justice more than you do. Believe me, it's all I've dreamed about for years. But my father's dead. Nothing's going to bring him back. And the rape… I've recovered from that." In a way. "We need to concentrate on getting your father out of jail while there's still time."

"Forget it."

"Rafe, come on. Be reasonable."

"I am being reasonable. He hurt you, and he's going to pay." His steely gaze held hers. "And I'm not changing my mind."

She stifled another sigh. "I appreciate the thought, but you don't have to avenge my honor. I'm doing fine on my own."

Rafe leaned forward, his face just inches from hers. "You shouldn't have to be on your own. I never should have walked away from you."

"I didn't give you much choice."

"I had a choice," he said, his voice even. "And I made a mistake. I can't go back and change that now but I can make sure Ortiz doesn't get off scot-free."

"And your father?" she challenged. "How can we abandon him?"

Rafe blew out his breath and sat back. He drained his glass, then shot her a brooding look. "Ortiz never intended to keep his word. Look how he framed us for that diplomat's death. As soon as we turn that ring over, we'll all be dead—you, me, *and* my father."

"We can't just give up. There has to be a way to help him."

"Not without some kind of leverage, something that will force Ortiz to keep his end of the deal."

Guilt warmed her face. "Like the flash drive I erased."

He nodded. "Whatever was on it must have been important if he's killing people to get it. So if we can find out what that is…"

They'd have a bargaining chip. Power.

Still feeling guilty, she broke off a chunk of cheese and nibbled the edge. "Maybe we should find a computer expert, someone who can recover lost data, and see if we can get it back."

"Yeah? Like who?"

"There's a guy who works for me who's pretty sharp. I could ask him to take a look at the flash drive and see."

Rafe shook his head. "It's too risky."

"We can trust him. I wouldn't have hired him if I wasn't sure."

He quirked a brow. "What about that message you couldn't find? How do you know he didn't do that?"

Her heart sank. Rafe was right. Someone had infiltrated her company's records and buried that message, and she had no idea who. "You have a better idea?"

"Maybe. I went to school with a guy. Miguel Calderón. A hacker. He might be able to help. I don't have his cell phone number, though. We'd have to go to his house and see if he's at home."

"Where does he live?"

"Up in the mountains. It's pretty remote, at least a four-hour drive from here." His frown deepened. "The ride could be tough on your ankle."

"But if he knows what to do…"

"There's no guarantee of that. And he might not even be home. It could all be a waste of time."

Time his dying father didn't have.

Gabi rose and hobbled to the broken window. The sun was sliding behind the mountains, stretching shadows across the fallow fields. She hated relying on anyone else. Ever since that attack, she despised giving up control. And asking this hacker to help them made them vulnerable. They had to trust him not to contact Ortiz.

But Rafe was right. They couldn't give Ortiz that ring unless they could force him to follow through. And with his father's life in the balance, they didn't have time to waste.

Rafe came up behind her, and she turned to meet his eyes. "All right, let's go see your friend."

"You're sure?"

"Yes. Like you said, we need power, and this is the only thing that makes sense."

Rafe nodded. "We'll head to his house at dawn."

"Why not go now?"

"Because we both need to rest. If we get too tired we're liable to make mistakes. Plus I need daylight to see the landmarks."

"Are you sure you want to wait? That article made it sound like your father's in pretty bad shape."

"Yeah, I'm sure. But Gabi…" His somber eyes fastened on hers. "No matter what happens to my father, we're going to get Ortiz. I promise. There's not a chance in hell he's going to win."

Her throat closed up. A heavy feeling pressed on her chest. And emotions tangled inside her—gratitude, relief, and something deeper, something far more stirring. Something she wasn't sure she wanted to name.

"I'm not worried about getting Ortiz," she admitted. "I just don't want anything bad to happen to you."

His dark eyes gleamed. The corner of his mouth kicked up, a feral grin slashing his whiskered face. "Don't worry. I can hold my own against him."

"I know that. It's just…he won't fight fair."

"Neither will I," he said, his voice rough. He reached out and cradled her jaw, and her pulse began to race. His thumb stroked down her throat, sending shivers rushing over her skin. His eyes turned even darker, more mesmerizing, the coal-black irises sucking her in.

He was going to kiss her. She knew that as clearly as if he'd shouted it out. And she knew that she ought to step back. Ortiz was hot on their heels. Rafe's father needed their help. This was the wrong time, the wrong place to think about kissing Rafe.

Then why did it feel so right?

Rafe shifted closer and bent his head. He paused, giving her time to pull away.

She couldn't move to save her life.

"Gabi," he said, his raw voice rumbling through her nerves.

"Kiss me," she whispered and wrapped her arms around his strong neck.

She didn't need to ask him twice. His iron-like arms banded her waist. He fused his mouth to hers. And the warm, firm feel of his lips jolted through her, welcoming her, sheltering her, as if she'd reached her long-lost home.

Forgotten needs unfurled inside her. Languid waves of pleasure rippled and danced through her veins. She plunged her hand through his short, silky hair, savoring the breadth of his muscled back, the strength of his powerful arms, lost in the glory of his embrace.

He tugged her closer against him, aligning her lower body to his. Then his warm tongue swept her mouth, awakening cravings deep inside her, sparking yearnings she'd stifled for years. Starved for his touch, she wriggled closer, desperate for the heat of his tawny skin, wanting to feel every delirious inch of his rock-hard frame.

He groaned against her mouth. The kiss turned primitive and wild, inciting needs she couldn't contain. An urgent moan escaped her, the feel of his arousal at the juncture of her thighs sending streams of desire coursing and shuddering through her blood.

But then the fierce excitement powering through her began to ebb. A sweat broke out on her brow, and she felt smothered, frantic, trapped.

Her breathing labored, she jerked away. Rafe lifted his head, confusion edging out the hunger in his eyes. "What's wrong? What happened? Are you all right?"

"I'm fine." Still gasping for air, she stepped away. "It's not you, it's just…since that attack I can't…" Despising her reaction, she shook her head.

"Gabi." He reached out, and she flinched back, unable to block the reflexive fear. He froze, his hand still outstretched. Then he slowly, carefully moved toward her, as if approaching a spooked animal, and tucked a stray strand of hair behind her ear.

"It's all right." His deep, gentle voice brought a lump to her throat. "Let's just get some sleep."

"Right," she whispered, her voice trembling, his patience gutting her heart.

He lowered his hand, gave her arm a reassuring squeeze, then returned to the table and poured himself more wine. She wrapped her arms around her belly and watched him, wishing that kiss could have ended differently, hating the effect Ortiz still had on her after all these years. He'd locked her in the dreadful past, trapping her in an emotional prison she couldn't escape.

But for the first time, she longed to try.

Chapter 10

The truth was a funny thing, Gabi decided as she rode behind Rafe on the scooter the following morning, clinging to his sturdy back. It wasn't always convenient. It certainly wasn't flattering. But it was impossible to ignore.

Rafe accelerated up the winding road, and she leaned closer against him, her eyes gritty from the lack of sleep. She'd passed a long, miserable night tossing and turning on the farmhouse floor, Rafe's scent and taste branded into her memory, alternating between unbearable longing and anxiety so strong that she'd been drenched in a chilly sweat.

And somewhere near dawn, as she lay listening to him breathe in the darkness, she'd finally stopped evading the truth. And she'd forced herself to confront the question she'd tried her best to avoid.

That rape had changed her. She was no longer the

carefree, uninhibited girl she'd been. Her conflicted reaction to Rafe's kiss proved that.

But now she had to wonder… Did those changes have
to be permanent? Could she regain what she thought
she'd lost? And even more importantly, was Ortiz really
trapping her in the horror of that night? Did he have that
much power over her?

Or was she doing that to herself?

She frowned at the forested hills whizzing by, not
wanting to answer that question, but far too exhausted
to sidestep the truth. All these years, she'd blamed her
problems on Ortiz—and rightfully so. He'd murdered
her father. He'd destroyed her idyllic life. She had every
right to hold him accountable for what he'd done.

But maybe somewhere along the way that consuming
need for vengeance had become a crutch. Maybe she'd
found it easier to focus on Ortiz rather than risk getting
hurt. Maybe those same self-preservation instincts that
had enabled her to survive the attack now hindered her
recovery instead.

Not pleased with that unflattering thought, she turned
her gaze to a glacier glinting on a distant peak. She
wasn't a coward. She always faced her problems head
on. But maybe after all these years she needed to look
at herself more critically.

And just maybe she needed to change.

Rafe shifted gears and slowed, then turned off the
two-lane highway onto a bumpy tractor path. Gabi
heaved out a sigh and leaned back, giving herself some
much-needed space. Rafe had done more than resurrect yearnings, more than render her unable to play her
seductress act. He'd forced her to face the naked truth

about her behavior—even if she didn't like what she'd found.

But she had too much at stake to spend time analyzing her life right now. First she had to help Rafe recover that missing data so they could defeat Ortiz. Then she'd deal with the fallout from that kiss.

Determined to maintain her focus, she scanned the timbered hillside for signs of the hacker's house. Half a mile later, she spotted a small, dusty SUV parked beside the trail. Rafe pulled up beside it and stopped.

"This is it." He cut the scooter's engine. "We'll have to hike the rest of the way."

She glanced at a narrow footpath leading through the dense stand of pines. "I'm surprised you found this place. I didn't see any signs."

"That's the idea."

She dismounted, her entire body stiff, and stretched her aching back.

"How's your ankle?" he asked as he set the kickstand and got off.

"Better." Although spending hours on the vibrating scooter hadn't helped. She straightened and met his eyes—and the unguarded hunger in those dark eyes shot a blast of lust through her veins.

So much for forgetting that kiss.

Shaken, she dragged in a tremulous breath, filling her lungs with the pine-scented air. "So you know this guy from school?" she asked, trying to conquer her wayward thoughts.

"Miguel? Yeah." Rafe started up the path. "His parents owned this place. I came here with him a couple times. I haven't talked to him in years, though."

"You're sure we can trust him?"

He turned around and glanced back. "As much as anyone, I guess. Why? Have you changed your mind?"

"No. We need his help. I'm just nervous."

"He likes to keep a low profile. I doubt he'd help the police."

Not exactly a ringing endorsement, but the most they could hope for right now.

Trying not to anticipate trouble, Gabi limped after Rafe up the trail. Several yards later, they reached the one-story house. Made of local fieldstone, it resembled a high-tech mushroom with dozens of satellite dishes and antennae crowding its corrugated tin roof.

Rafe loped up the wooden steps and knocked on the door. Gabi continued more slowly, trepidation weighting her steps. How could this hacker afford that kind of equipment? Was trusting him a mistake? Or was stress skewing her judgment, making her suspect an innocent man?

A tall, lanky man in his early thirties answered the door. Dressed in jeans and a wrinkled T-shirt, Miguel Calderon was an attractive man with a dark goatee, trendy, black-framed glasses, and keenly intelligent eyes. He pretended not to recognize her, but she knew at once that he'd followed the news.

Rafe made short work of the introductions, and they stepped inside. While he gave Miguel a summary of recent events, Gabi scanned the computers stacked around the room, the cords and wires running over the hardwood floor like twisted vines.

"Can you retrieve the data?" Rafe asked, getting straight to the point.

"Let's see the flash drive."

Gabi dug it from her pocket, then hesitated, reluctant

to give it up. But that was silly. They needed this man's help. She shoved her qualms aside.

Miguel studied it for a moment, then pushed his glasses up the bridge of his nose. "Did the Americans know this was stolen?"

She shot Rafe a questioning look. "I suppose so. Once their diplomat turned up dead, they must have realized it was gone. Why do you ask?"

"This type of flash drive has some top-notch security features. One of them is a silver bullet."

"Meaning?"

"Meaning they can wipe the data. They can enter a command remotely, sending a message to the flash drive to self destruct. As soon as someone hooks it up to an internet-ready computer, it triggers the command."

She turned that over in her mind. "But I didn't enter the password. And it said I'd have ten tries."

"That's different. This is a separate security feature they can activate to make it self-destruct. As soon as you inserted it into the USB port, it started to work."

She blinked at that, impressed. "Wow. That really is high tech. But what about the deleted files? Is there a way to recover them?"

"No. They're definitely gone. These flash drives are the best there is. That's why the Americans used it."

Her hopes tanked. "So there's nothing we can do?"

Miguel handed the flash drive back. "Not unless there's another copy somewhere."

Rafe's forehead creased. "I found it next to the police chief's laptop."

Gabi shot him a glance. "You think he made a copy?"

"Who knows? He might have decided to see what was

on the flash drive, assuming he knew the password. So it's possible, I guess."

"But wouldn't that have triggered the silver bullet? I only had it in the computer for a few minutes before it deleted the files."

"Not if he wasn't connected to the internet. Or maybe he looked at it before the Americans gave the command to delete it."

And maybe they were grasping at straws.

Miguel's gaze swiveled from Rafe's to hers. "You want me to hack into his computer and check his hard drive?"

Gabi's pulse picked up. "Could you? It's a lot to ask. You might be in danger if you do."

Miguel flashed her a grin. "I'm up for the challenge." He headed toward a bank of computers beneath a large picture window overlooking the hills. "It might take a while, though, so make yourselves at home. Kitchen's that way. Bathroom's down the hall."

Rafe took the seat next to Miguel, and the two men got to work. Gabi dithered for a moment, too restless to sit and watch. But as she wandered the room, searching for something other than computer manuals to read, her gaze kept boomeranging to Rafe—his strong, corded neck, those shoulders wide enough to support the world, the muscles of his powerful arms…

Disgusted at her obsession, she headed to the bathroom, found a clean towel stuffed in a closet, then took a hot, heavenly shower and shampooed her hair. But no matter how hard she tried to block them, no matter how many other worries swirled around in her mind, her thoughts kept returning to Rafe. Could she regain her lost sexuality after all these years? Should she try?

She flushed, her entire body heating at the images that provocative thought evoked—the erotic sweep of his tongue, the flex of his rock-hard muscles beneath her hands, the thrills he'd torched, sending pleasure quivering and skidding though her veins.

She shivered, certain about one thing. If she did want to take the plunge, Rafe was the ideal man. There was no one she trusted—or who excited her—more. And from the hunger she'd glimpsed in his heated eyes, she doubted that he'd resist.

She snapped off the faucet and grabbed the towel. Making love to Rafe was a major step, a decision she couldn't rush. She'd be opening herself up to those memories, that fear she'd repressed for years. And what if it didn't work? What if she couldn't get over the past? What if it triggered the nightmares she'd tried so hard to forget? She'd end up more depressed, more frustrated, more vulnerable.

And right now she had more important problems to deal with. Because if they didn't defeat Ortiz they'd both be dead.

The men were still absorbed in the computer when she returned, their low voices and the soft clicks of the keyboard breaking the silence in the small room. Resolving to keep her mind off Rafe, she headed into the kitchen, then made an egg and potato tortilla for lunch.

She'd just cut it into slices when Rafe called out. "Gabi! Come here. We're in."

The food instantly forgotten, she rushed to his side. Miguel tapped several more keys, and an old, black-and-white photo appeared on the screen.

"This is it," Miguel told them, rising. "Ortiz saved a copy on his laptop. He was sloppy and didn't encrypt it, luckily for us." He stepped aside, and Gabi scooted into his vacated chair.

She held her breath, anticipation making her heart thud. This really was it—her chance to discover why Ortiz had murdered the diplomat, to find out if she'd been right.

She leaned forward, her head close to Rafe's as she studied the screen. The photo showed a dozen teenagers standing in a hayfield, holding rifles and wearing berets. Two younger children gripping a banner knelt in front of the lined-up teens. In the background, the bell tower of a village church peeked above the trees.

Rafe pointed to the hand-lettered sign. "*Morior invictus.* Reino Antiguo's slogan. This must be a *La Brigada* youth brigade."

Gabi's pulse sped up. *La Brigada* was the terrorist arm of the separatist movement, responsible for numerous kidnappings, bombings and deaths. "Can you enlarge the photo?"

Rafe clicked on the screen and zoomed in. Gabi studied the teenagers' faces, her excitement rising as recognition dawned. "Good grief. This is a Who's Who of terrorists. Look." She pointed to one of the boys. "Iñaki Zurbano." She moved her finger to the girl at his side. "His sister, Maite, *La Brigada*'s chief bomb maker. Gaspar Serrano, Paco Roig. Rosa Heras." She moved her finger across the screen. "All known terrorists." All major players in the organization. All deadly criminals bent on destroying the government of País Vell.

Her gaze stalled on a tall, thin boy standing in the back, a little off to the side, and a cold fist squeezed her heart. "Oh, God," she whispered, a dull buzz filling her ears.

Rafe leaned closer. "Is that—"

"Yes." She hugged her arms. She would recognize those empty soulless eyes, no matter what his age. "Raymundo Ortiz."

"Damn." Rafe's shocked gaze cut to hers.

She stared back, the implications staggering. The head of País Vell's security—the king's right-hand man—was a terrorist.

This news was explosive. It would rock the foundations of País Vell. No wonder he wanted to destroy the proof!

"How about these two?" Rafe asked, drawing her gaze back to the screen. "You recognize them?" He pointed to the two skinny children holding the sign.

Still boggled at what they'd discovered, she peered at the barefoot boys. "No. But the rest…"

Dizzy with disbelief, she slumped in the chair. She'd known all along Ortiz was a traitor, but a *terrorist*… And he was in charge of protecting the king! She pressed her hand to her throat, grappling with the shocking news.

"But why would he save this?" she asked. "This photo will ruin him. You'd think he would destroy the evidence, not save a copy on his hard drive."

Rafe shook his head. "Who knows? I'm just glad he did. At least now we have some power."

He turned to Miguel, who stood behind them, his grim gaze on the screen. "Can you make a copy of this for us?"

"We'd better make more than one," Gabi said. "We don't want to risk losing it again."

"I'll copy it to a couple flash drives and save it online," Miguel said. "Then I need to cover our tracks.

His computer might have a trip wire that can trace my IP address."

Gabi cringed. He was right. If Ortiz knew Miguel had seen this photo, he wouldn't let him survive.

"You need to leave the country," she told him. "Fast. I'll give you money. You need to hide until we can fix this thing."

Because suddenly, their mission had changed. Not only did they have to liberate Rafe's father, not only did they have to prove Ortiz killed her father *and* the American diplomat...

They had to warn the king.

But how?

Gabi was still trying to find an answer to that question as they parked Miguel's SUV beside an abandoned barn that evening. They'd decided not to risk returning to Reino Antiguo, given the police chief's separatist ties. Instead, they'd borrowed Miguel's truck, loaded it with supplies, then traveled the back roads of the Pyrenees Mountains, getting as close as they dared to the village of País Vell.

"I still say we should contact the prime minister," she said, carting a bag of food into the barn.

"What makes you think we can trust him?" Rafe ducked through the doorway behind her, then closed the wooden door.

"He runs a spy network to root out traitors. I think he's a pretty safe bet."

"And if you're wrong?"

She set the food on a wooden plank along one wall and crossed her arms. The temperature had fallen as the sun went down, cooling the mountain air. "I'm not wrong. I've known him all my life."

"People aren't always what they seem."

"I know that." Her father had led a secret life. She'd concealed that rape for years. Even Rafe's family had obscured their real activities, working as cat burglars behind the scenes.

"We don't even know for sure what that photo means," he continued, setting a bundle of blankets on the board. He picked up the lantern they'd borrowed and turned it on. "It's forty years old. Ortiz might not have anything to do with the terrorists now."

"He wouldn't have killed that diplomat if it didn't matter. Or my father, either."

"You don't know that's the reason he killed him."

"No." She was making a leap. "But I doubt Ortiz has that many secrets he's willing to kill for. And if he wants to hide this photo, he must still be involved with the terrorists somehow."

Rafe set the lantern on the board and rose, the low light accentuating the angles of his face. "All right. Let's assume you're right about Ortiz. The prime minister could still be involved."

"I don't see how. He got me invited to the reception. He's been working with me all along."

His eyes flashed. "Right. And look what happened. You nearly ended up killed."

"That wasn't his fault." Exasperated, she huffed out a breath. Why did Rafe persist in suspecting the prime minister? He'd never doubted her judgment before.

She frowned at him in frustration, studying the mulish set of his mouth. And suddenly, she understood.

He was worried about her safety. He was trying to protect her from harm.

Touched, she walked over to where he stood. "Look, Rafe. I appreciate what you're trying to do. But I can't back out now. And I don't want to. I made a promise to my father and I have to see it through."

He folded his arms across his chest. "I don't want you to get hurt."

"I know that. I don't want anything to happen to you, either. But we're in this thing together—no matter how it turns out."

He shook his head. "I still don't want to involve the prime minister. There are too many things about this we don't know."

"I don't think we have a choice. We can't get near the king. The guards will shoot us if we try. They think we killed that diplomat, remember?"

"Yeah."

"And if we try to reach the king by phone, we'll just get an assistant who'll tip off the guards. The same thing goes for email or anything else we try."

Still looking reluctant, Rafe stalked to a nearby window and stared out at the gathering night. "So what do you suggest?"

She hitched out her dammed-up breath. "We can't call the prime minister, for the same reasons. Ortiz could monitor his calls in case we try to contact him. And it won't do any good to go to his house. Tonight's the end of the G-6 summit. They'll have a dinner and meetings until late, so he'll probably stay in town."

"That doesn't leave many options."

"No." She thought hard. "But he stops at his office

every morning. If we get there early enough, maybe we can avoid Ortiz."

"Assuming we can get past the guards. And even then, we don't know that he'll help. He could turn us over to Ortiz."

"I know it's a risk." Guilt slivered through her, making her conscience twinge. She was asking a lot of Rafe. He was going to have to trust her. He would have to rely on the prime minister, a man he didn't know. And he'd be handing over that photo, the only leverage they had over Ortiz.

She crossed the dirt floor and joined him at the window, then gazed out at the glittering stars. An owl hooted in the darkness. The cool breeze gusted, blowing through cracks in the glass. Rafe stood silently beside her, his dark eyes brooding, tension emanating from his muscled frame.

But then he speared his hand through his hair and sighed. "Have you been to the prime minister's office before?"

"A few times with my father. It's in the old monastery at the *Plaza Mayor*."

He turned his head, meeting her gaze. "Can you draw a floor plan and point out the exits?"

She thought back. "I think so. On the main floor, at least. I'm not as sure about the second floor."

He turned his face again to the window, his brows drawn into a frown. The tinny clanking of cowbells drifted in from the distant hills. "All right," he said at last. "We'll do it."

"You're sure?"

He snorted. "Hardly. But if you think he's reliable, I'll take the chance."

Her heart softened, bringing a rush of warmth to her chest. He trusted her. He was setting aside his distrust of authority, overlooking her past deception and taking a leap of faith. He was risking everything—his life, his father's freedom—with no guarantee of success.

Maybe it was time she did the same.

Nerves fluttered in her belly. She took a deep breath, her thoughts rushing back to that kiss—and the question she'd been dancing around all day.

She'd shunned all intimacy since the rape. She'd stayed stalled in that moment of horror, trapped in the past, so careful to protect herself from further harm that she'd never broken free.

But she needed to move on, to put that attack behind her for good. And Rafe could help her heal.

If she had the courage to enlist his help.

She snuck a glance at his strong, masculine profile, the power in his bulging arms, and her pulse tapped in chaotic beats. He'd taken the leap to trust her. Was she brave enough to do the same?

He tilted his head and met her eyes. And even in the dim light she could see his carefully banked hunger, the desire shimmering in his eyes. And something unraveled inside her, a feeling of tension letting free.

And she knew without a doubt that this was right.

"You'd better rest," he said, his voice suddenly gruff. "We'll head out before dawn."

"I don't want to rest." She stepped closer, her heart slamming against her rib cage, her throat suddenly parched. "I want you to make love to me."

Chapter 11

Rafe stood motionless before her, his silence deafening, looking as if he'd lost the ability to breathe. Gabi's courage quickly fading, she forced herself to explain. "The thing is, after that attack, I couldn't...I haven't... Not since I was with you. I—"

"Gabi—"

"No, listen. I need to say this." Before her nerve completely fled. "I get panicked. Like last night when we kissed. And I hate it. I hate that I'm still stuck there, that it affects me after all these years. I need to let it go."

"But Gabi—"

"Unless you don't want to." The words rushed out in a burst of uncertainty, and she searched his eyes. "Maybe it was presumptuous of me to ask. But I thought...that

[...] puffed out a strangled laugh. "I want to. You have no idea how much."

He stepped even closer, his [...]

"Then please." She stepped closer, his warm, masculine scent filling her senses, her heart beating fast enough to take flight. "I know it's a lot to ask. I might not…it might take time. But I need to do this, and I…I want you. I trust you."

His eyes burned into hers. He shifted closer, his broad shoulders filling her vision, and her heart beat quicker still. "You're sure?" His voice came out deep and gruff.

"Yes," she whispered. "I'm absolutely sure."

The muscles worked in his corded throat. A pulse point ticked in his jaw. He reached out and tucked a loose strand of hair behind her ear, the tender gesture reassuring her that he was safe.

"What do you need me to do?" he asked.

She inhaled, nerves gathering in her belly at the step she was about to take. "I don't know. Just…take it slow, I guess."

"You'll tell me if you need me to stop?"

"Yes."

His dark eyes stayed on hers. Her heart banged against her chest. He traced the line of her jaw with his thumb, the light caress raising goose bumps along her spine, making it hard to breathe. Then he gently cradled her head with his hands, worshiping her face with his gaze as if she were a treasured work of art.

"Do you have any idea how beautiful you are?" he asked, his low voice rumbling inside her, sparking a maelstrom of sensual flutters, and she closed her eyes on a sigh.

This was going to be all right. She had nothing to fear from Rafe. She no longer had to pretend, didn't have to put on an act. She could trust him to do the right thing.

He stepped even closer, his hard thighs brushing hers,

his solid chest grazing her breasts. She held her breath, expecting an onrush of panic, but desire flooded inside her, a languid stream of longing that heated her blood.

Then he lowered his head, and his firm, warm lips covered hers in a kiss. Her heart ramped up its beat. Her body burst to life, long-buried sensations erupting like fireworks in her veins. She inhaled his masculine heat, his enticing woodsy scent wrapping around her, the provocative rasp of his jaw arousing her more.

His hand came around her waist. He pulled her closer against him, taking possession of her mouth, and she opened to him with a sigh. She scooted nearer, every thought driven from her head, her world narrowing to this one man.

He kissed her slowly, leisurely, as if nothing else existed except this kiss. But her hunger began to build. She wrapped her hands around his neck, the hard muscles of his shoulders bunching beneath her hands, his coiled strength reassuring her that she still had control.

Her mind turning fuzzy, she arched against him. His long, drugging kisses reeled her in deeper, a sensual whirlpool she didn't want to escape. She needed this. Needed him.

Shivers raced over her skin. Her knees weakened, her body moistening, an insistent craving rising inside. And suddenly, she needed desperately to feel him, to have his warm, callused hands on her naked skin.

He broke the kiss and raised his head. His uneven breath dueled with hers. Hunger burned in his jet-black eyes. She couldn't move, couldn't tear her gaze from his. This was the man she'd loved forever. The man who made her feel safe, daring, desired.

She stepped away and tugged off her shirt. His

eyes followed the movement, lingering on her swollen breasts. She unlatched her bra, but hesitated on a sudden spurt of insecurity, doubts clamoring in the back of her mind.

But this was Rafe. He wouldn't hurt her. She had nothing to fear from him. She sucked in her breath and peeled her bra away.

His low, rough sound of approval banished her doubts. He closed the distance between them, then hauled her into his arms, the tremors racking his powerful body encouraging her more. Feeling brazen, she swept back her hair, giving him access to her pouting breasts, her nipples pebbling hard for his touch.

And then he bent his head, one hand clamping her against his arousal as his hot mouth ravished her breast. She clutched his hair, consumed with the building pleasure, a throbbing ache pulsing between her legs.

He scorched a fiery path up her throat, then took her mouth in another kiss, urgent now, insistent, mimicking the hunger she felt inside. She melted against him, lost in the delirium, never wanting the pleasure to end.

His big hands cupped her bottom, causing a frenzy of need to break loose inside her, and she let out a throaty moan. Then he lifted her, carried her to the blankets, and set her down. He tore off his clothes, scattering them over the ground, while she made short work of her jeans.

She stood before him naked, exposed, the cool air puckering her nipples, further shivers chasing over her skin—bringing her crashing back to reality and resurrecting a sliver of fear.

But he tugged her down to the blanket with a growl. In a swift powerful movement he pulled her beneath him, his steely muscles flexing, his arousal prodding the juncture of her thighs. Her body throbbed for him, moistened for him, weeping for the pleasure she'd denied herself for years. This was Rafe. She'd be all right. She—

No.

He rose and loomed above her. Her breath abruptly caught, a tight, smothered feeling invading her chest. *Not now!* She squeezed her eyes shut, fighting it, not wanting the panic to win. Rafe would never hurt her. She had no reason to fear. She grasped at the pleasure rapidly slipping away.

But panic erupted inside her. Rafe lowered his weight, trapping her against the blanket, and the desperate need to escape exploded inside. She needed air. Space. She shoved on his chest to get free.

He jerked up his head and blinked, his eyes heavy-lidded with hunger, arousal tightening the planes of his dusky face. "What's wrong?"

"Stop," she pleaded, gasping for breath. "I can't…you have to stop." Growing frantic, she flailed against him, but she couldn't get him to budge. He was too big, too heavy, too male. Hysteria surged inside her, hot tears springing to her eyes.

He rolled off her with a groan and lay flat on his back beside her, covering his eyes with his arm. He was fully aroused, his breath ragged and hoarse, his skin glistening in the golden light.

Her heart racing, she labored for air, any remnants of pleasure shattered, trying desperately to calm down. "I'm sorry. I can't… I hate this feeling. I'm so *sick* of it. But I don't know how to stop it. I feel suffocated, scared."

Several seconds passed. Rafe passed a hand down his stubble-roughened cheeks, then turned his head to meet her eyes. "What exactly scares you?"

Trembling, she tugged her knees to her chest, drawing her long hair over her breasts. "I think it's…losing control." Fear threaded her voice. "I feel…vulnerable. Trapped. Like I don't have any power. That was the worst part, knowing he was going to kill me, that no matter how hard I fought, no matter what I did, I couldn't win." She closed her eyes, trying not to relive the horror, refusing to go back to that dreadful place.

"Gabi."

She dragged open her eyes, Rafe's soothing voice bringing her awareness back to him. "What?"

"It's all right. You just need to be in control." Still lying on his back, he placed his palms on the ground. "What if I don't touch you, if you do everything—as fast or slow as you want?"

Her breath caught. Her eyes stayed locked on his. "You think that will help?"

"I won't touch you unless you ask. I promise. You can do whatever you want, at your own pace."

"You can do that?"

His mouth crooked up, forming sexy brackets in the beard stubble covering his jaw, and her heart gave a sideways lurch. "I might die in the meantime, but yeah, I can do that."

"All right," she agreed, intrigued with the thought.

She lowered herself beside him. He closed his eyes, his dark lashes resting against his tanned cheeks, and broad muscles swirled in his own. Whenever they'd made love, Rafe had always taken control. His dominant streak had thrilled her, his demands provoking her to exciting heights.

But now... If she wanted to defeat those memories, *she* had to take the initiative. She had to seize control.

Suddenly feeling awkward, she traced the sloping planes of his cheekbones, the virile angle of his jaw, the frown lines etched in his brow. She studied his blatantly carnal mouth, the sexy hollows at the base of his throat, the beautifully sculpted muscles of his arms.

The lantern light flickered, bathing his skin in a tawny glow. Reassured, she raised herself on an elbow and continued her exploration, stroking the bulging curve of his shoulders, the veins in his sinewed forearms, admiring the play of shadow and light on his sculpted chest.

He looked less threatening lying down—definitely not weak, and not exactly gentle—but less menacing somehow. She ran her hand down his abs, over the hard, flat muscles of his belly, and her pulse began to pound.

His eyes opened to slits. "You know you're killing me here."

Warmth slid around her heart. Her mouth kicked up, her confidence returning in spades. "Sorry about that."

He grunted and closed his eyes. Emboldened now, she retraced a path up his muscular arms, over the flat nipples on his chest, to the dark hair arrowing down his abs. Her breath grew shallow and fast. Desire again beat in her veins.

She hesitated, her gaze fastened on his face, then reached even lower and took him into her hand. His eyes remained closed, but he clenched his jaw, his irregular breathing betraying the effort it took to stay still. But he kept his promise and didn't move, encouraging her even more.

She rose and straddled his hips, then fused her mouth to his. He growled then, his deep, ravenous kiss proof of the hunger he was trying to restrain. Her own urgency mounting, she positioned herself above him, then paused.

"Protection," he ground out. "In my wallet."

"Right." She reached for his jeans, quickly took care of the condom, then guided him to her warmth. He gritted his teeth, sweat beading his brow, the muscles bunching along his jaw. She lowered herself slowly, inching over his rigid shaft, until he was hard and thick inside.

Then she stopped. She felt no fear, no panic, just pleasure so fierce she wanted to burst. "Rafe," she breathed.

He groaned and fisted his hands. "If you don't move, I'm going to explode."

Needing no urging, she started to rock. Rafe's glazed eyes stayed locked on hers, his stark, blatant hunger setting off a maelstrom of need. She picked up the pace, finding the ancient rhythm, the rasp of his breath, the savage heat in his eyes spurring her on.

Sharp desire fisted inside her, hunger so strong she wanted to scream. She moved faster, harder, writhing against him, her frustration and urgency mounting, grasping for the pinnacle lying just out of reach.

She had to let go. Let loose. Let the frenetic need consume her. But she couldn't abandon control. Her desperation grew.

"Rafe," she pleaded, but he kept his word and didn't touch her, a low groan his only response. Her breath came in ragged gasps. Tears formed behind her eyes. She couldn't...she couldn't...

And then she tensed, her entire body rigid, torrid pleasure lashing her like a sensual whip. She tipped back her head and let out a keening cry, shuddering as stars burst behind her eyes. And wave after wave of exquisite pleasure roared through her, a tsunami of carnal bliss.

Rafe broke down and gripped her hips. He gave a few hard thrusts, then joined her over the edge, his deep shouts mingling with hers.

Tears leaked from her eyes. Aftershocks continued to splinter through her. Euphoria rose as the delirious spasms began to subside.

She lowered herself over Rafe's chest, and he reached up and grasped her head, taking her lips in a deep, grinding kiss that seared her soul.

Then he rolled her over, pulled her against his side, sheltering her in his arms. She lay panting beside him, feeling ecstatic, liberated, *free.* She stroked the sculpted muscles of his chest, tracing the sinews and veins beneath his skin. He was an utterly beautiful man—and not just physically. He was patient, potent, exciting. Everything she'd ever desired.

She closed her eyes, afraid he'd see her feelings verging perilously close to a place she couldn't go.

"Are you all right?" he asked. He dabbed at the tears streaking her cheeks.

"Perfect." Better than she could express. Rafe had healed her, releasing her from the terror of the past, helping her regain the physical pleasure she'd repressed for years.

Not that making love had solved their problems. Terrible danger still plagued them. They had to save Rafe's father before he died. And Ortiz could find them at any time.

But at long last she'd recovered her sexuality. Rafe had helped her conquer her fear.

She sighed, relishing the comforting warmth of his body, the sound of his rough breath deepening in sleep. She opened her eyes and gazed at his rugged profile, happiness bubbling inside.

It would be so incredibly easy to love this man. She admired everything about him—his loyalty, his honor, his willingness to fight for justice.

And physically… She'd never found a more perfect match.

But she couldn't involve her heart—not with Rafe, not with anyone. She'd changed too much for *that*. Ortiz's brutal assault had done more than make her afraid of men. It had shattered her dreams, her belief and trust in authority, destroying any idealism she'd once had.

Sex was one thing. But love… She didn't have that in her anymore. That attack had deadened something inside her, turning her empty and brittle inside.

And the last thing she wanted was to lead Rafe on. She'd hurt him enough in the past. She needed to pull back and resurrect the boundaries between them before this affair got out of hand.

But not yet. She closed her eyes, savoring the security she felt in his arms. And for the first time in years, she felt at peace.

A soft sound woke Rafe before dawn. He lay unmoving on the hard dirt floor, his dreams giving way to a parade of sensual memories—Gabi standing naked, her lush mouth hot on his. Her provocative scent wrapping around him. The caress of her silken hair. Her siren eyes drawing him closer. Her sleek breasts pouting for his touch. And when she'd taken him inside her...

His lower body throbbed. His blood running heavy, he reached out his hand to touch her, but only grasped empty air. Disgruntled, he opened his eyes.

She stood in the darkness by the window, the first stirrings of dawn tingeing the sky. He took in the tension of her fully-dressed body, the distance she'd put between them, the clothes folded and stacked at his side.

So that was how she intended to play it. She was backtracking, pretending nothing had happened, that the intimacy they'd shared didn't exist. Not sure why it mattered, he narrowed his eyes.

She turned, as if sensing his scrutiny. Their eyes connected across the shadowed room. She clasped her hands and looked away. "Listen—"

"Don't," he said.

Her gaze snapped back to his. "Don't what?"

He sat up. "Don't start analyzing last night. Don't try to explain it away. And don't pretend it never happened, because it did."

Her chest rose as she inhaled. She hunched her shoulders and crossed her arms. "I know it happened. And I enjoyed it. A lot. More than I can say. But now—"

"Now what? We forget it?" He tossed aside the blanket. Her gaze dropped to his blatant arousal, and she spun to face the window again. He pulled on his clothes, his anger growing with every breath.

He hadn't expected a declaration of love. Truthfully, he didn't know what he'd wanted from her this morning; he'd been too caught up in the urgency and the delirium of her body to think that far ahead.

But he'd be damned if she'd shut him out.

He shoved his feet into his shoes and tied the laces. Then he balled up the blanket and stuffed it into a bag. "What exactly do you want from me, Gabi?"

She turned to face him again, and the vulnerability in her eyes caught him off guard. "I don't know," she whispered, her voice uncertain. "Just…we need to turn in that photo."

"Right." Still battling his temper, he raked his hand through his hair. He knew he was overreacting. She'd been through a terrible ordeal which had left her feeling spooked. And this anger simmering inside him was probably due to his wounded ego. He still wanted her, *badly,* and she didn't seem to care.

But he should be glad she was backing away. They had no future together. He wasn't the naive man he'd once been. That belief that love conquered all, that he could overcome any obstacle—wealth, education, class—if he cared about her enough had disappeared years ago.

He'd grown up. He knew how the world worked now. And they had different goals, different careers, different lives. No matter how mind-blowing the sex had been, they couldn't resurrect what they'd lost.

She crossed the room and picked up the bag of food, her eyes not quite meeting his. "I drew a map," she said, handing him a rolled-up paper. "Of the prime minister's office. We should probably leave before it gets light."

"Fine." He tossed her the keys to the SUV. "You drive while I study the map."

"All right." She shot him a hesitant gaze, then started for the door.

"But Gabi…"

She paused. He stalked toward her, watching the uneasiness mount in her eyes. "Running away isn't going to change what happened."

"I'm not running. It's just…we need to hurry. Ortiz could catch up at any time."

"If you say so." Still feeling ticked off, he stopped beside her, so close he could see the flecks of gold in her eyes. Then he reached out and touched her cheek.

Her eyes turned even more cautious. Tension shimmered from her slender frame. He stroked his thumb down her satin skin, unable to stem the hunger still burning inside him.

"I don't know what last night was about," he admitted. "Maybe it meant nothing. Maybe you were using me. Maybe it was just temporary insanity for us both. But I do know one thing."

"What?" she whispered, her wary eyes on his.

"From where I stand, you're still running scared."

Chapter 12

Gabi drove the SUV toward the village of País Vell, her thoughts skittering from the upcoming meeting with the prime minister to her argument with Rafe in the barn. She knew she'd bungled the "morning after." No doubt she'd hurt his feelings when she'd refused to discuss their affair.

But no matter how ecstatic he'd made her feel, last night hadn't been real. It had been a moment out of time, a hiatus from the crazy turmoil of their lives. They had no relationship, no future; they might not even survive the next few hours. *That* was their harsh reality. And acknowledging that fact just made her practical; it had nothing to do with fear.

The SUV crested another hill. She snuck a look at Rafe slouching beside her with one muscled arm planted on the armrest, his jean-clad legs spread wide. Her gaze roamed from his thick, black hair and whiskered throat to the enticing stress marks on his faded jeans.

Far too tempted to reach for him, she tightened her grip on the wheel. Real or not, last night had been spectacular. But it was over. She had to stop obsessing about Rafe. She definitely couldn't wallow in the memories— the erotic scrape of his jaw, the thick feel of him pulsing inside her, the shattering waves of bliss.

Her face burning, she cracked open the window and gulped in the cool morning air. She had to focus. They were about to turn over the photo and throw themselves on the prime minister's mercy, putting their lives at risk. Mulling over the nuances of her relationship with Rafe would have to wait.

Without warning, he sat upright. "Pull over."

"What?"

"Stop! Right here."

Startled, she swerved off the two-lane road and slammed on the brakes. "What's wrong?"

"There's a roadblock ahead. Didn't you see it?"

"No." She'd been too busy looking at him. "Where is it?" She peered at the road ahead, but they'd descended into a valley, and she couldn't see over the hill.

"It's right at the edge of town."

She tensed. "You think they're looking for us?"

"I don't know." His eyes met hers, torching a surge of lust in her veins, but she quickly tamped it down. She had to concentrate. Her inattention could get them killed.

"They had bomb sniffing dogs," he added.

"Dogs?" She frowned at that. The summit had ended the previous night. The diplomats would already be leaving town, meaning the guards should be cutting back on security, not adding more. Unless…

"The king. He's giving a speech today in the *Plaza Mayor*." Horrified, she stared at Rafe. "What if that's Ortiz's plan—to attack the king?"

Rafe's brows gathered. "Why would he do that?"

"The separatists despise the royal family. You know that. If they can get rid of the monarchy, they might gain independence from País Vell."

"But why do it *now?*"

"Why *not* now? The king's vulnerable any time he gives a speech. And if Ortiz is working with the separatists, he could help them pull it off."

Her mind raced, but her sense of certainty grew. "I'm right, Rafe. I know I am. We have to warn the king." It was even more urgent now. But if Ortiz had the roads blocked off, how could they get into town?

A truck sped by, then disappeared over the hill. Gabi stared at the empty road, frantically flipping through options, trying to figure out how to get in. "We can take that path again, the one we followed when we left town."

"We don't have time. Without the scooter, we'd have to hike, and that could take hours."

And by then the king could be dead. "Then what do you suggest?"

He rubbed his bristled jaw. "You feel up to acting?"

"What do you have in mind?"

"You saw that truck go by."

"So?"

"So with all the activity in town, there'll be more trucks heading in, more deliveries to the restaurants and bars. When the next one comes by, you pretend to have car trouble and get the driver to stop. Once I've disabled him, we can use his truck to get into town. They'll have to let a supply truck through."

"Disable him *how?*"

He quirked a brow. "What do you think?"

She reared back in her seat. "No, forget it. I don't want anyone else to get hurt." That diplomat was bad enough.

"We wouldn't hurt him, just tie him up until we can get into town."

"No." They'd broken into Ortiz's palace. They'd stolen that scooter, clothes and supplies. But involving another innocent person in this… "There has to be another way."

"Like what? We need some kind of cover. We can't just waltz into town with our faces plastered all over the news. We'll never make it past that roadblock. And no one's going to help us. They'll turn us in to collect the reward. At least with a delivery truck we have a better chance to get through."

"I don't see how. They'll recognize us no matter what kind of truck we're in."

"Not if we disguise ourselves. You must know some tricks from your acting days. And if we get lucky, we'll find a driver with a uniform I can use. That will help throw them off."

She grimaced. "I don't know. It seems too obvious."

"We don't have much choice. There's no other way to get in."

And they were fast running out of time.

Still balking, she frowned out the windshield. A hawk soared over the trees, silently hunting the woods for prey. *Like Ortiz.* Her blood chilled at the thought. "It still feels wrong to steal a truck."

"I know." His quiet voice drew her gaze, and she saw the reluctance in his eyes. "But so does getting killed."

And if they died, so would the king.

She kneaded the dull ache gathering between her brows. But Rafe was right. They had to warn the monarch fast.

She heaved out a sigh. "You're right. We have to do it. But you have to promise to be careful. I don't want anyone hurt."

Suddenly all business, Rafe reached into the back seat and grabbed one of the blankets they'd brought. Then he took out a pocketknife and cut it into strips. "I'll head back to that last hill and watch the road. You stay here in the car for now. As soon as I see a truck, I'll wave. Pop the hood, then get out and flag it down. Pretend your car stalled. I'll take care of the rest."

She nodded, still not thrilled with the plan, but what alternative did they have?

He handed her a strip of cloth. His coal-black eyes held hers, and her belly flip-flopped, whether from dread or aftershocks from the torrid night, she couldn't say. Then he opened the door and got out.

She swiveled in her seat and watched him jog through the woods to the top of the hill. A moment later a car drove by. Another went past several minutes after that. Gabi trained her gaze on Rafe, trying not to worry about what lay ahead. But the stakes couldn't be higher—to themselves, the king, even the future of País Vell.

Rafe waved.

Her heart stumbling, she unlatched the hood on the SUV and jumped out. She hurried around the front, propped open the hood, then leaned against the driver's side door, clutching the strip of cloth.

A white panel truck crested the hill. She watched it approach, her stomach fluttering as Rafe ran back through the woods. The truck began to draw close. She raised the cloth and flagged it down.

The driver pulled off the road and got out. He was perfect, a bit shorter than Rafe and stockier, but maybe with a little padding… And he wore a dark blue shirt and uniform hat bearing a nearby vineyard's name. The man smiled as he headed toward her, his ruddy cheeks marking him as a local, and her conscience suffered another pang.

But they were doing this for the greater good.

"Good morning," the man said, his eyes friendly. "What's the problem?"

She didn't need any skill to act distressed. Her guilty conscience took care of that. "I don't know. It just stopped. I think…it might have been leaking oil."

He frowned. "That's not good." He peered at the engine and scratched his jaw. She stayed to the side, praying he didn't notice Rafe creeping toward them through the woods. "Have you checked to see how much oil it has?" he asked.

"No, not yet. I was looking for a cloth to wipe the dip stick off." Rafe appeared in her peripheral vision, sneaking up on the SUV. She handed the man the strip of cloth and edged away.

The man leaned farther under the hood. In a move so fast it shocked her, Rafe sprang out and kicked him behind his knees. Then he spun him around and threw a strike to his head. The man staggered and collapsed on the ground with a moan.

Horrified, Gabi covered her mouth. "Is he all right?"

"He'll be fine."

"But—"

"Open the side door." Rafe stripped off the man's shirt and pulled it on, then jammed his cap on his head. He searched the driver's pockets, divesting him of his wallet and keys, then gagged him and bound his hands.

"I'm so sorry," she told the man as Rafe hefted him over his shoulder in a fireman's carry. "We just need to borrow your identity for a while. It's important. If you watch the news later, you'll see why."

Rafe unloaded him on the SUV's backseat. Then he rolled down the window for air; "Come on," he said. "Let's get out of here before someone sees us." He jogged to the driver's side of the truck.

Still filled with remorse, she shot the good Samaritan an apologetic look. "I'll make up for this. I promise," she told him. Then she hurried to the truck and climbed in.

"You'll have to hide in the back," Rafe told her. "They'll be watching for a couple. And you're too easy to recognize."

"What about you?"

He opened the truck driver's wallet and examined his license. "I'll be Pepe Alonso. As long as the guards don't look too hard at his photo, I should be all right."

"They won't have to look at it. They'll recognize your face from the news. You need a better disguise."

Glancing around the cab, she spotted a first-aid kit at her feet and pulled out a roll of gauze. "Here. Stuff some of this into your cheeks. That'll change the shape of your face. And see if you can find some rags to pad your shirt."

While Rafe tried to make himself look heavier, she found an old pair of glasses in the glove compartment and handed them to him. Then she studied the first-aid kit again. "How about a bandage? People tend to notice things like that."

Rafe's forehead creased. "I thought the point was to avoid attention."

"Exactly. They'll pay more attention to the bandage than they do to you. Later, when they go to describe you, they won't remember your features, just the wound." She shrugged. "I know it sounds too simple, but it really does work."

He lifted one broad shoulder. "It's worth a try."

She took a bandage from the first-aid kit and turned his way. Slanting her head, she studied his dark, slashing brows, his basely sensual mouth, the desperado beard stubble coating his jaw, and her heart began to thud. "We'll put it on your left cheek," she decided. "That's the most noticeable spot."

Rafe leaned toward her and angled his head. She peeled open the bandage and smoothed it over his cheekbone, his warm scent curling around her senses as she worked. Her hand brushed his jaw, the erotic feel of his whiskers electrifying her pulse.

Her breath caught, a torrent of sensual memories rippling through her, prompting a rush of lust. Her breasts turned tight. Sudden warmth flooded between her legs. Her gaze locked on his, and the blatant hunger in his eyes slammed through her, making it impossible to breathe. "That's the best we can do," she heard herself say. "As long as they don't look too closely…"

"You'd better get in the back," he said, his voice rough.

"Right." Trying desperately to recover her focus, she climbed into the narrow space behind the seats and curled up on the dirty floor. She couldn't think about the past night. She had to concentrate on saving the king. Rafe tossed a blanket over her back, then piled cardboard boxes on top.

"Are you all right?" he asked.

She grimaced. Hardly. "I'll survive." *She hoped.*

The engine rumbled to life. Rafe accelerated onto the road, the floor vibrating beneath her as they climbed the hill. "The roadblock's just ahead," he warned. "So don't move. I'll let you know when we're safely through."

The road leveled off. Her pulse sped up as the truck began to slow. They came to a stop, and she held her breath, every second an eternity as she strained to hear what was going on.

"Where are you going?" a man asked.

She couldn't distinguish Rafe's answer, just the deep murmur of his voice. She prayed he could pull this off, that the guards wouldn't recognize him from the news— or notice her hiding behind the seat.

The truck's rear doors rattled open. Exhaust fumes seeped through the floorboards, the truck rocking slightly as the guards walked through the cargo hold. Tension mounted inside her, making her want to scream. What if they searched the cab of the truck?

Then the doors slammed shut. *"Vale,"* the guard said. "Let him through."

Rafe shifted gears, and the truck lurched into motion again. She eased out a shaky breath, thankful for his nerves of steel. The truck rattled harder as they drove onto the cobblestone road.

"You can come out," Rafe said, turning a corner. "We're in the village now."

Relief billowed through her. She threw off the boxes, then crawled back into the seat. "Do you think the guards suspected anything?"

Rafe took off the cap and glasses, then dragged his hand through his hair. "I don't know. It seemed almost too easy."

Dread flickered through her. Had Ortiz anticipated their actions? But how could he know what they'd planned?

She frowned at the street crowded with people, her apprehension growing as they neared the *Plaza Mayor*. She'd insisted on this plan. She'd convinced Rafe to trust her judgment. If anything went wrong it would be her fault—and innocent people could die.

They rounded a corner, then drove up a bustling side street, braking every few yards for the people spilling across the road. Rafe made a sudden turn into an alley and stopped. "We'd better get out here. We're not going to make any progress with these crowds." And if the guards had recognized Rafe, they needed to hurry and ditch the truck.

"All right." Her uneasiness mounting, she opened the door and hopped out. Rafe removed the uniform shirt and joined her, and they hiked up the narrow street. A motor scooter buzzed past. A television blared in a nearby bar. The crowds increased as they neared the plaza, their noisy chatter and festive air at odds with her rising nerves.

"We'll never get into the plaza," Rafe said, bending his head close to hers. "It's already too crowded, and the guards will have the area around the stage blocked off. We'd better try the back."

They detoured into the alley behind the plaza, then approached the prime minister's office—a former medieval monastery that formed one corner of the ancient square. Gabi scanned the imposing three-story building with its fortress-like turrets and adjacent bell tower. A royal guard stood sentinel at the rear door.

Rafe pulled her behind a Dumpster, and they both peeked out. "Let me do the talking," she said, keeping her voice low. "I'll convince the guards to let us see the prime minister. He'll protect us from Ortiz." *She hoped.*

Because this was it. Once they approached that guard, they couldn't conceal their identities. They'd be recognized, arrested, held as prisoners until the prime minister sorted things out.

She caught Rafe's eye, the grim determination on his face adding to her doubts. She wasn't only risking her own life, but his. Trying to quell her sudden panic, she swallowed hard. "Listen, Rafe, if anything goes wrong—"

"Nothing's going to go wrong. We're going to be fine."

She held his gaze, knowing he was trying to reassure her by minimizing the danger they faced. A ribbon of warmth unfurled inside her, a sudden thickness blocking her throat. She'd never met a more heroic man.

"Are you ready?" he asked.

Her heart faltering, she nodded. Striving for a courage she didn't feel, she rose and led the way toward the guard, knowing the next few minutes would determine their fate.

The guard whipped around at their approach. His

eyes widened, his Adam's apple bobbing in his throat as he gaped at them, obviously recognizing them from the news. But then he raised his rifle, and they stopped.

For a long, tense minute, no one spoke. Gabi's palms moistened with sweat. The roar of voices from the plaza filled the air. Then the guard barked into his radio and called for backup. Within seconds, a dozen armed guards streamed out the monastery door, surrounding them.

She swallowed hard, praying she'd done the right thing.

Because no matter what the outcome, they were committed now.

A short time later, Gabi found herself locked in a third-story turret with Rafe. She paced restlessly across the former library, her steps echoing on the stone floor as she battled a barrage of doubts. But she must have done the right thing. Her father had trusted his cousin, so she could, too. And the prime minister was loyal to the king. He would have to help them, given the damning proof they'd found.

She glanced at Rafe standing by the balcony doors, his strong back rigid as he gazed out at the plaza below. Iron grilles covered the glass, blocking access to the balcony, making it impossible to escape.

They were trapped, all right—the balcony barricaded, the thick, wooden door to the hallway barred from the outside, an armed guard standing watch.

More uncertainties swarmed inside her. She kept thinking that she'd missed something vital, some sort of clue hovering just beyond her reach. But she had no reason to worry. Nothing bad would happen to them.

She just hoped she'd convinced the guards to notify the prime minister instead of Ortiz. The king was scheduled to speak in another hour.

Still trying to calm herself, she made another circuit of the room, glancing at the religious fresco on the vaulted ceiling, the glassed-in bookcases filled with leather books, the photographs of village churches along one wall. The guards couldn't have chosen a more secure location to hold them, she'd give them that much. Not only was the turret impossible to escape, but snipers watched from surrounding rooftops, poised to protect the king.

Just then the door to the hallway opened, and she whirled around. The guard came in, followed by the prime minister, and her breath rushed out in relief.

"Arturo," she said, hurrying toward him. "Thank God they called you in time."

"Gabrielle," the prime minister answered with a smile. "At last. I've been worried about you."

"I almost didn't make it. This is Rafael Navarro, by the way. I'm sure you recognize him from the news."

The prime minister nodded at Rafe, his heavy jowls quivering, his bald head glinting in the light. But Rafe only crossed his arms and scowled back.

Neither man spoke, and she hurried to fill the gap. "I found the proof we wanted." She glanced at the guard standing beside the prime minister, hesitant to let him hear. The police chief's power was extensive. He probably had spies among the guards. "But we need to speak in private," she added.

"Certainly." The prime minister turned to the guard. "Wait for me outside."

The guard stiffened. "Sir? These prisoners could be dangerous."

"Gabrielle is my cousin. I assure you she isn't a threat."

"But—"

"I said I'll be fine," he repeated, his voice steely. "Now wait for me in the hall."

The guard's expression went blank. "Yes, sir." He pivoted on his heel and left.

The thick door thudded closed. Arturo gave her an apologetic shrug. "Sorry about that. The king's speech has put everyone on edge. Now what did you want to say?"

"We have the ring and the intelligence we were after," she said. "We were right, by the way. It incriminates Ortiz."

Pulling one of the copies of the flash drive they'd made from her pocket, she handed it to him. "There's a photo on it. It shows him as a teenager at a separatist training camp. The other people in it are all terrorists— prominent members of *La Brigada*. There's no question about it. And that means the king's life is at stake."

"I see," Arturo said, his expression grim. "I'll warn him at once."

"Good." She crinkled her brows, something niggling her memory, but she shook the worry aside. "We also need you to protect Rafe's father. He's in prison. Ortiz has already made an attempt on his life."

"Of course. I'll put people on that right away. You said you have the ring?" He stretched out his puffy hand.

"It's not here," Rafe said. "We've put it in a safe location with another copy of the photo. We'll turn them both over after we've warned the king."

Gabi shot him a look of surprise. Was he bluffing? Or had he hidden it without telling her? He obviously didn't trust the prime minister—but why?

Silence drummed between them. The prime minister kept his gaze on Rafe. "Good thinking," he finally said. "We can worry about getting it later."

He turned back to her. "You'll have to stay here for now. Not long, just until we arrest Ortiz. It's the best way to keep you safe."

She frowned, hating the thought of sitting by idly with the monarch's life at stake. But he was probably right. Ortiz's men would shoot them if they left the room.

Pocketing the flash drive, he strolled over to the wet bar along the wall. "Can I get you something to drink before I go? I can have food brought up, as well."

Gabi glanced at Rafe, but his scowl only deepened. "No, we're fine," she assured him. "Just hurry and warn the king. It can't be long now until his speech."

"Don't worry. I have everything under control."

The prime minister wandered over to the photos, his lack of urgency making her belly tense. Didn't he realize the monarch's life was at stake? "Listen, Arturo—"

"Do you recognize this?" He pointed to a photo of a church.

Her impatience mounting, she shook her head. "No, but you need to tell the king—"

"Take a closer look."

"Fine." Exasperated, she walked over and glanced at it, the twelve-sided Romanesque structure striking a chord. "It's the Knights Templar church." The one near the farmhouse where she'd hidden with Rafe, near the estate where she'd grown up, near Arturo's childhood home, too.

"Exactly." His eyes reflected his approval. "It's the one in the photo."

The photo? Her head jerked up. He was right. She should have recognized that. "But how did you know..."

He whipped out a pistol and pointed it at her head. "Drop it," he barked to Rafe.

Stunned, she gaped from the barrel of Arturo's gun to Rafe, who was suddenly holding his pocketknife—which he'd somehow concealed from the guards.

"I said to drop it," the prime minister ordered again.

His eyes thunderous, Rafe dropped his pocketknife on the floor.

"Now kick it over here, or she's dead."

Rafe's jaw like granite, he complied.

His gun still aimed at her, the prime minister bent and picked up the knife. Then he shifted his gaze to her. "I'm surprised you didn't figure it out. But I guess I've changed a lot since then. I was only ten."

When she still didn't get it, he raised a brow. "The banner?"

And suddenly, her heart stopped cold. *Of course.* The prime minister was one of the children holding the sign. He'd changed dramatically over the years—balding and putting on weight—which explained why she hadn't recognized him.

Which meant he was a terrorist, too.

"Bravo." He smiled. "I knew you'd finally figure it out. And I have to thank you for making my job so much easier. I couldn't have gotten the photo without your help."

Still unable to believe it, she stared at the man she

thought she'd known, a numb feeling spreading inside her. He was a terrorist. He was working with Ortiz. He'd betrayed the king, his country, *her father*.

"You," she gasped. "You were the one who had him killed." A terrible feeling of betrayal lodged in her gut. "But why?" she asked. "Why would you kill him? And why would you join the terrorists? It doesn't make sense." Arturo had built his career fighting *La Brigada*. He was the most pro-monarchist man she knew. He had power, prestige, influence with the monarch. "What could you possibly have to gain?"

He gave her a sardonic smile. "Money, what else?"

"But you're not poor."

"Not now. But I was. My father squandered everything we had."

She struggled to digest that. She'd heard rumors about his father, a notorious gambler, but she'd never thought… "But why join up with the separatists? What does money have to do with them?"

"They control the smuggling routes. They're the ones with all the power in País Vell. Everyone knows that. And I knew I'd need their help to get rich. That's why I joined the youth brigade."

"You're saying you planned all this as a child?"

His eyes turned hard. A mottled flush stained his cheeks. "I was hungry. When you face a lifetime of poverty it doesn't take long to form a goal. And it wasn't fair. I saw how your father lived. I wanted the lifestyle I deserved."

"Fair?" Her voice trembled with outrage as the ramifications set in. "You killed my father. How was that *fair*?"

"He should have minded his own business. I wasn't

hurting him. But he threatened to report us to the king. And I wasn't about to lose everything I'd earned."

She recoiled in disgust. "So you had Ortiz murder him."

"I had to. We had too much at stake."

"And the king?" Rafe asked, inching closer. "Why kill him now?"

The prime minister raised his pistol, causing Rafe to stop. "He's trying to out an end to the smuggling. The Americans, the European Union—they're all pressuring him to crack down."

Gabi's heart lurched. "So you're going to assassinate him."

"You are, actually. At least that will be the story. You're working with the separatists. That's where the ring comes in. We uncovered the plot and had you arrested, but not in time to stop the bomb. Unfortunately, you'll get shot while trying to escape.

"I'll be outraged, of course," he continued. "I had no idea my cousin was a traitor."

"And the separatists?" Rafe asked, his voice flat. "What do they get out of this?"

"Nothing." Arturo grinned. "That's the irony of it. They think I'll convince the crown prince to grant them independence, but they're idealistic fools. I'm not giving up that income yet."

A knock came from the hall. Keeping his weapon trained on them, Arturo walked over and opened the door.

"Sir," the guard said. "I'm sorry to interrupt, but Señor Ortiz is on his way."

"I'll be right out."

His eyes returned to hers. "Ortiz will deal with you shortly. He likes that type of work, you know."

He went out the door, and the bar dropped into place, the stark finality dealing a death knell to her hopes.

Gabi hugged her arms, horror rising inside her, appalled by her mistake. She'd naively trusted the prime minister and played right into his hands. She'd involved Rafe, overriding his better judgment, endangering the one man she'd sworn to protect.

And now there was no way out.

Chapter 13

The sound of the bolt slamming home galvanized Rafe. He strode to the door, thoroughly disgusted at his stupidity, and pressed his ear to the wood. He'd suspected they couldn't trust the prime minister, so he'd hidden the ring in the barn as a safeguard, convinced it would guarantee them access to the king.

But he'd been a fool. Neither Ortiz nor the prime minister cared about that ring. They only needed to keep that photo hidden until they'd done away with the monarch to keep their profits intact.

And now here he was, trapped in a cell-like turret with hundreds of lives hanging in the balance—the king's, Gabi's, his father's, the innocent people in the plaza below....

What was he going to do?

"I'm so sorry." Gabi's voice trembled. "I never should have believed him. I had no idea—"

"Shh." He motioned for her to be quiet. "It's not your fault. There's no way you could have known. Let's just concentrate on getting out of here before they kill the king."

Leaning against the door, he tried to decipher the men's deep voices, but the thick plank muffled the sound. Gabi joined him at the door, her worried eyes fastened on his.

"Where did the guard go?" the prime minister suddenly asked, and Rafe realized he'd moved closer to the door. "He's supposed to stay here until we get back."

"There's been a change of plans," Ortiz answered.

"What change?" Suspicion rang in the prime minister's voice.

"This." The blast of a gunshot thundered through the hall.

Rafe jerked away from the door. Gabi stumbled toward him, her face devoid of color, her wide eyes mirroring his shock. He pulled her close, his mind whirling, a profound silence ringing in his ears.

Ortiz had just shot the prime minister. What the hell was going on?

Gabi's body quivered hard. She lifted a trembling hand to her mouth. "Oh, my God," she whispered. "What happened? Did he kill him?"

"That's my guess." And Ortiz probably planned to shoot them next.

His jaw hardening, he pushed Gabi behind him and faced the door. Ortiz might intend to kill them, but he wasn't going to succeed. Rafe was going to protect Gabi, no matter what it took.

But Ortiz's footsteps faded away. Stark silence descended on the hall. Rafe turned around and met her eyes. "Ortiz is gone. The prime minister must be dead."

Her face blanched even more. "I don't understand. If they were working together, why would he kill him?"

He shoved his hand through his hair, just as perplexed. "Who knows? A power struggle?"

A cheer rose from the plaza outside. Frowning, Rafe followed Gabi to the balcony windows and peered through the iron bars.

"The king must have arrived," she said. "Can you see anything?"

"Not yet." Spectators leaned out the windows of the surrounding buildings. Every balcony was jammed. The ancient square was wall-to-wall people, cheering and waving flags. Rafe shifted, angling for a better view, and searched through the crowd near the stage.

And then he saw them. The king. The black sheep princess, Paloma. Prince Tristan, the only surviving son and heir to the throne.

His heart plummeted, dread taking hold in his gut. "It's not just the king. It's the entire royal family."

Gabi paled. "He's going to kill them all." Her voice was hoarse with shock.

And suddenly it made sense. With the royal family gone and the prime minister dead—supposedly at the separatists' hands—Ortiz could declare martial law. He'd seize control of the government, crack down on any rebellion, and assume absolute power.

"He's staging a coup," Rafe said, his voice tight with anger. "We've got to warn the king."

But how? The door was barred from the outside, the balcony blocked off. And even if they could get out there, the noise was deafening. No one would hear them shout. Worse, anything they did to attract attention would alert the snipers on the surrounding roofs.

He glanced around the room, but there was no chimney, no ventilation shaft, only a small, fixed window near the roofline that he doubted he could squeeze through.

But he was going to try. "Help me move the desk over to the wall," he said.

Gabi glanced up at the window. "You think you can fit through that?"

"I'd better."

She raced to the desk and grabbed one end. Rafe lifted the other, but Gabi couldn't get hers to budge.

"Let's take out the drawers," he said.

They yanked them out and tossed them aside, not worrying about the damage or noise. Then they grabbed the desk again. "Now!" They just managed to lift it, enough to keep it from catching on the uneven stones, and lugged it across the floor.

"That's good," he said, shoving it into position against the wall. Then he grabbed the wooden desk chair and set it on top of the desk. "You'd better stand back. I need to break the glass." He grabbed a heavy metal stapler and scrambled up.

Working quickly, he punched out the glass and knocked away the loose shards. The pieces shattered again as they hit the stone floor. Hurrying, he tossed the stapler to Gabi and took hold of the window frame, his arms and shoulders bunching as he tried to squeeze through the narrow space. But he couldn't wriggle through.

"Damn."

"What's wrong?" Gabi called from below.

"It's tighter than I thought." Grunting, he tried again. Sweat stung his eyes as he twisted, determined to get himself through. But his shoulders were still too wide.

"The window's too small," he said, lowering himself to the chair.

"I can do it."

"Forget it." Breathing heavily, he jumped to the floor.

"Why? My shoulders are narrower than yours. I'm sure I can squeeze through."

He wiped the sweat from his eyes with his sleeve. "The roof has clay tiles. They're slippery as hell to walk on, and it's a three-story drop from here."

"But—"

"Gabi, there are guards posted all around. They've got snipers on the opposite buildings. If they see you, they'll shoot to kill."

"As opposed to what? Waiting for Ortiz to kill us here?"

She braced her hands on her hips. "Someone has got to get out there. And if you were going to risk it, why shouldn't I?"

"I've been climbing across roofs my whole life."

She blew out her breath, making the loose hairs flutter around her face. "I'll be careful. Believe me, I don't want to die. But we've got to get out of this room."

He shook his head, unwilling to let her do it. Everything inside him rebelled at the thought of Gabi crawling across that roof. But damned if she wasn't right.

"I can get through that hole," she insisted. "Just help me up there. It's the only chance we have."

He plunged his hand through his hair, his instincts clamoring to keep her safe. He'd never felt as frustrated—or helpless—in his life.

But they didn't have another option. If they didn't escape within minutes, the royal family would die.

And they'd be next.

"All right," he said, reluctance pulling at his voice. "When you get out there, head to the dormer window. It's only a few yards away. If you can't get it open, break the glass." He nodded to the metal stapler. "Once you're inside the building, come right back and open the door." He pinned his gaze on hers. "I mean it, Gabi. You have to let me out. Don't try to warn the king on your own."

"I will. I promise."

"And for God's sake be careful. Those tiles are slick."

Emotions surging inside him, he reached out and pulled her close. Then, unable to help himself, he claimed her mouth in a hard, punishing kiss, giving vent to his worry, his frustration, his need. Making a primitive stake of possession, a no-holds-barred declaration of love.

He loved her.

He abruptly ended the kiss, the realization barreling through him like a runaway truck. He loved her. He'd never stopped. She was his perfect mate, the woman who drove him insane with lust, the woman he respected, admired, adored.

And now he might lose her for good.

Her head still spinning from that ravenous kiss, Gabi climbed up on the desk beside Rafe. What on earth had that been about? He'd never kissed her like that before— urgent, merciless, almost angry in its intensity—sparking a frenzy of desire in her blood.

Shivering, she eyed the window. Whatever the cause, she didn't need the distraction. Bad enough that the prime minister had just been killed. Worse that the fate of País Vell rested on her slender shoulders, that the royal family was about to die in a bomb blast unless she could make it over that roof.

Anxiety thrummed inside her. Scaling heights with Rafe was one thing, but with no safety equipment, no one there to protect her, and a three-story drop to certain death below...

She pushed that terrifying thought away. She could do this. She *had* to do this. She'd caused this mess, now she had to get them out.

Which meant she had to stop thinking about that mind-bending kiss.

"Stand on the chair," Rafe told her. "Then climb onto my shoulders. That should get you close enough. If you can't do that, I'll lift you up."

She scrambled onto the chair, stuffed the long, heavy stapler into her back pocket, then stretched and grabbed the ledge. Balancing, she put one knee on his broad shoulder and pulled herself toward the window, shifting her weight fully to him. He gripped her legs to keep her steady, and she stuck her head outside.

Bright sunshine beat on the roof tiles. The roar from the crowds below filled the air. Summoning her courage, she rose to her feet and twisted her shoulders through the narrow opening. Rafe gave her a boost, and she crawled onto the roof.

Panting, she glanced around. The dormer window lay straight ahead, a dozen yards across the steep roof. Her gaze swept the red clay tiles angling downward to the plaza three dizzying stories below her, and a blast of vertigo swamped her head.

Oh, God. She closed her eyes, a sudden rush of

nerves freezing her in place. But she had no choice. She had to get to that dormer window fast.

Trembling, determined not to think about falling, she fastened her gaze on the dormer window and started crawling across the tiles. Cheers and hollers erupted below her. Perspiration dripped down her spine. Afraid to stand, she crept across the uneven ridges and gutters, her hands and knees aching, until there were only a few feet left to go.

Suddenly a tile beneath her knee broke loose. Thrown abruptly off balance, she slipped, lost her grip, and started sliding down the roof. She let out a panicked shriek.

Total terror gripped her. She grabbed at the tiles, frantic to find a handhold, but her hands were slick with sweat. A wild frenzy erupted inside her. Desperate, she clutched at the tiles, trying to dig in her feet and break her momentum, but she kept bumping and skidding toward the edge.

Then her fingers found purchase on a broken tile. The ragged edge gouged her hand, but she clung to it with a death grip, finally managing to halt. She gasped and heaved for breath, too horrified to look behind her, knowing she was just inches from falling to her death.

A tiny whimper escaped her. Her limbs started shaking, threatening to loosen her grip. She cautiously probed with her toes, wedged her foot into a narrow ridge, then slowly pushed herself upward, away from the lethal edge.

Her entire body trembling, she crawled to the dormer window. Then, grabbing the edge of its roof like a lifeline, she blinked back tears, her courage completely gone. But she still had to get inside.

She slanted a glance toward the window—a mere two feet from the edge of the roof. Trying not to hyperventilate, she closed her eyes and gathered her resolve. Then she shifted around and banged on the glass, but it refused to budge.

Knowing she had to hurry, she pulled the stapler from her back pocket, then leaned out further and hit the window again. The frame gave way, the aged latch shuddering beneath the strain. Encouraged, she struck harder, and the hinges broke off. Another blow pushed the window inward and it fell to the floor with a crash.

Her breath tumbled out in relief. But now came the hardest part—crawling through the window without falling over the edge.

Inhaling deeply to focus, she reached around and gripped the edge of the open window, trying to keep her mind off the plaza below.

But then the tile shattered beside her head.

She reared back, suddenly confused.

She scanned the empty rooftop. Then a movement on the building across from her caught her eye. A guard stood on the roof with a rifle—aimed right at her.

All thoughts of the precarious edge forgotten, she lunged around the dormer and dove through the open window, just as a barrage of bullets hit the tiles.

She crashed to the wooden floor, landing amidst a pile of broken glass. Her adrenaline surging, she jumped to her feet and whirled around.

She was in a small, dusty room with a water-stained ceiling, the old servant's quarters gone to ruin. She rushed to the door and threw it open, then darted down the narrow hall.

That sniper would alert the guards. She only had seconds to rescue Rafe. She reached a short flight of stairs and leaped to the bottom, then flung open another door.

She was back in the hallway outside the library. Her gaze arrowed instantly to the body slumped in a pool of blood on the floor. *The prime minister.*

A wave of bile threatened to choke her, but she forced herself to move. She raced down the hall to the library, skirting his unmoving body, then pried the bar off the door.

"Rafe," she called, entering the room.

He stepped out from behind the door and froze. "You're bleeding."

She glanced at her arms, now sticky with blood, and realized she'd cut herself when she'd landed on that glass. "I'm fine, but a sniper saw me."

Rafe's expression turned even grimmer. "Let's go." He followed her into the hall and lowered the bar on the door so nothing appeared out of place. Then they hurried down the hall, heading the way the guards had brought them in. But the sound of approaching voices stopped them cold.

"Damn. This way!" Rafe grabbed her hand and pulled her through another doorway to the side. He shut it behind them, and she spun around.

They were in the chapel's choir loft. She glanced at the rows of wooden seats, the dim light filtering through the stained glass windows above, and her desperation rose. There was no way down.

Rafe peered over the railing. "You stay here. I'll drop down and warn the king."

"But—"

"There's no time. I'll come back for you later."

Before she could argue, he climbed over the railing.

He dangled for a moment off the edge, then let go, landing on the floor with a heavy thud.

"Are you all right?" she called down.

"I'm good." He leaped to his feet and darted off.

"Be careful!" she called, but he was gone.

An oppressive silence closed around her. Still breathless, she scanned the chapel below her—the empty pews, the altar shrouded in darkness—and anxiety clawed at her nerves. How was Rafe going to warn the king? The guards would shoot him if he got too close. And what if he didn't make it in time? Or what if he did—and the bomb went off?

Chilled, she pressed her arms to her belly, ill at the thought of the carnage that bomb would inflict. She couldn't just stand here, doing nothing. She had to warn those people in the plaza before they lost their lives.

Turning around, she studied the choir loft. She couldn't climb down. And she couldn't return to the hall with the guards fast closing in.

She spotted a staircase going up to the belfry, the discovery making her pause. Maybe she could climb up there and ring the bell. It might get the people moving before Ortiz detonated the bomb.

Knowing every second counted, she rushed to the spiral staircase but a wooden barricade blocked it off. Ignoring it, she climbed over top and started up the old stone steps.

She saw the reason for the barricade at once. The ancient stairs were cracking and crumbling, pebbles breaking away beneath her feet. She swallowed hard, refusing to worry about the steps. If she'd made it across the roof, she could manage this.

The stairs continued winding upward. Her breath

growing labored, she trailed one hand along the rough stone wall. The air turned colder, the noise from the crowds in the plaza louder as she neared the top.

She finally reached the bell-ringing room and stopped. Trying to catch her breath, she glanced around. Several thick ropes—connected to the bells above— dangled in the center of the room. Sunlight streamed from the openings the ropes passed through.

With no time to waste, she grabbed the nearest rope and pulled—but it took more strength than she'd thought. She pulled even harder, her arms and shoulders straining, her palms growing slick with blood and sweat. The wheel operating the bell creaked, then turned, and the bell began to ring. The metallic noise rocked through her skull.

Praying that the people would scatter, that they'd understand there was an emergency, she continued to work the rope. But what if they didn't get it? What if they thought the bells were part of the celebration to welcome the king? She needed to make them run.

Abandoning the rope, she raced to the wall, then started up the wooden ladder toward the bells. She reached the sound chamber the ropes passed through, paused to wipe her slippery palms on her jeans, then continued climbing up. The ringing slowed to a stop. She made it to the bell tower, stepped out between the bells, and looked down at the cheering crowd.

"Bomb!" she shouted. "There's a bomb! Danger! Run!" She waved her arms, trying to attract attention, but there was no way anyone could hear her, no matter how hard she screamed.

Frustrated, her sense of urgency rising, she saw the

royal family standing on the stage. Rafe was out there, lost somewhere in the excited crowd.

And a bomb was about to go off.

Desperate, she hurried back down the ladder and resumed ringing the bell. If nothing else, the noise would keep the king from starting his speech, giving Rafe a chance to warn him about the bomb.

The pealing bell deafened her ears. Seconds turned into minutes, but she refused to stop. Then an explosion rocked the church, the force knocking her off her feet. She hit the floor, the blast echoing through her skull, stones tumbling from the cracking walls. She flinched as they struck her back.

Dazed, she rose to her knees. The bells clanged crazily above her. The temblors shuddered to a stop.

Pushing herself upright, she staggered to the stairs, panic spurring her on. Where was Rafe? He had to be alive. She'd never forgive herself if he died.

Her ears still ringing, she stumbled down the staircase, desperate to get to Rafe. Seconds later, she reached the choir loft and stopped.

A man blocked her way, holding a gun.

Ortiz.

Chapter 14

Ortiz's mouth slashed into a smile. His sadistic eyes bore into hers with that cruel, crazed gleam that had haunted her nightmares for years. She whirled on her heels and fled, sprinting back up the spiraling staircase, pure panic powering her flight. But there was nothing above her but the bell tower—or a deadly plunge to the plaza below.

Aware she was out of options, she continued her frantic race upward, sending loose stones skittering and crashing in her wake. She leaped the final distance to the platform where the ropes hung and searched for a way to escape.

But there was no way out. She either had to scale the ladder to the bell tower or stay and confront Ortiz. Behind her, his footsteps pounded the stones.

Then she noticed a small, wooden door behind the

dangling ropes. Praying for a miracle, she rushed over and yanked on the door.

It didn't budge. Frantic, she heaved on the door again, and it opened with an angry squawk. She lunged inside and slammed it shut behind her, but there was no lock, no bolt, no way to keep the police chief out. Pivoting, she realized she'd entered the triforium, the passageway that encircled the nave, overlooking the chapel two stories below.

Knowing Ortiz was just seconds behind her, she sprinted down the narrow hall. She rounded the corner, then tore down the opposite corridor, the open archways passing by in a blur.

When she reached another corner, she slowed. She was running in a circle—heading straight back to Ortiz. *Where was the staircase to the floor below?*

Without warning a gunshot rang out. Terrified, she sped up, desperate to get out of the line of fire. But another shot blasted behind her, and a sharp burn tore through her arm. She stumbled and nearly fell, then skidded into the corner and turned.

Her lungs seared as she struggled to stay upright. She ran to the end of the corridor and doubled back toward the bell tower—but the passageway dead-ended in a mountain of stones.

The bomb blast had caved in the walls. She spun around, searching for an escape route, but there wasn't any way down. She peered through the arched openings running the length of the triforium, but she'd die if she tried to jump.

Hysteria swarmed inside her. Blood streamed down her fiery arm. Ortiz's footsteps thundered closer, obliterating her hopes. In seconds, he'd shoot her dead.

Wide-eyed, she stood waiting, trapped before the pile of rubble like prey he'd run to ground—helpless, cornered, vulnerable.

The feeling she most despised.

But then anger ignited inside her. Ortiz had murdered her father. He'd probably killed the royal family and Rafe. And there wasn't a chance in hell she'd stand here cowering and let him win. She was done living in fear. Done being his victim. Done watching him kill the people she loved.

Maybe she wouldn't survive. Maybe he'd murder her in the end—but she was taking him with her if he did. She refused to die without exacting justice. *She'd had enough.*

She picked up a rock from the pile behind her. Resolve settling deep inside her, she lugged it back to the corner and flattened herself to the wall. She'd have one shot, one chance to knock him off balance, one opportunity to disarm him and get away. She couldn't fail.

Her breath clammed up. Icy sweat trickled down her spine. His footsteps thudded closer, louder, and then they slowed.

Time ground to a halt. She stood motionless, her ears straining, every second stretching into eternity, her entire life winding down to this one crucial moment in time.

Ortiz or her. Only one of them was going to survive. Her vision tunneled, animal instincts taking over. The scent of her terror filled the air.

Ortiz turned her way. She hurled the rock at his head. It glanced off, and he stumbled sideways, losing his grip on the gun.

She dove to the floor and snatched it up just as he

regained his feet. He swung his head toward her like a bull, fury burning in his eyes.

But now she had the gun.

He paused. His gaze traveled from the gun to her, and then a taunting smile twisted his lips.

He started stalking toward her. She backed up, but the pile of rubble blocked her path. She had no way to escape—unless she killed Ortiz.

He continued moving closer. Her arm trembling, her strength ebbing, she steadied the gun. "Stop right there."

"Or what? You'll shoot?" Amusement filled his eyes. "You don't have the nerve."

She gritted her teeth and hardened her voice. "I said to *stop*." She aimed the gun at his heart.

He shook his head. His eyes brimmed with that same gleeful malevolence as when he'd squeezed the life from her throat. "You won't do it. We've got unfinished business between us. And I do intend to finish it, Gabi." He let out a giddy laugh.

She squeezed the trigger and shot. The recoil sent her staggering backward, the blast roaring through her skull. She fell, landing on the rocks, the acrid stench of gunfire filling her lungs.

She jerked up her head. Ortiz took another step forward, and she gaped in disbelief. She'd just shot him. He should have died!

Then surprise lit his eyes. He looked down at his chest where a red spot began to form, and dropped to the floor with a thud.

Silence blanketed the hall.

Gabi struggled to her feet, still gripping the gun. Then she slowly approached him and stopped. And for a long moment she stared down at the man who'd terrorized her life. She felt no relief. No anger. No sense of triumph or justice. Nothing. Just numbness that he was finally dead.

Rafe charged down the medieval hallway, the reverberations from that gunshot echoing in his ears. He skidded around a corner, the king's guards hard on his heels, then raced flat-out down the hall.

That bastard was after Gabi. He knew it with brutal certainty. He'd caught a glimpse of Ortiz near the chapel, but he'd been too busy trying to reach the king to head him off. He'd dispersed the crowd and warned the guards, who'd whisked the royal family to safety seconds before the bomb went off.

Not everyone had escaped. Several bystanders had lost their lives. And Ortiz had disappeared in the pandemonium of the bomb blast, skittering away like the cockroach he was.

But Rafe would be damned if he'd let him win.

He rounded another corner, then abruptly came to a stop. Gabi stood over Ortiz, holding a gun—her face ashen, her T-shirt soaked with blood. Ortiz lay crumpled at her feet.

And suddenly, Rafe couldn't breathe. "Gabi," he croaked out, dizzy with fear. *"You've been shot."*

The guards continued running past him and surrounded Ortiz. Gabi handed a guard the gun, then slowly began walking toward him, her gait unsteady, her skin a pasty white.

"He's dead," she announced needlessly.

His heart erratic, he rushed to her side. "Forget Ortiz. Where did he get you?"

"My arm. But I'm fine." She twisted to see her biceps, and her face turned chalkier yet. "It's nothing, really."

He zeroed in on her tattered flesh and panic mushroomed inside. "We've got to get you to a hospital."

"No, I'm all right. But you…" Her eyes looked huge in her bloodless face. "You made it."

"Yeah." He shot a scowl at the guards talking in their radios. "We need an ambulance here!"

"And the king?" Gabi asked, her voice growing weaker.

"He survived, The whole family got away in time."

"Good." She closed her eyes.

"Gabi." His heart fisted. Stark fear slashed through his nerves. He lunged forward and caught her as she wobbled on her feet.

Then she fainted dead away.

Several hours later, Gabi perched on a bed in País Vell's royal hospital, ready to leave. The doctors had pumped her with fluids, then cleaned and stitched her arm, shooting enough painkillers into the wound to render it blessedly numb.

She wished they'd done the same to her heart.

The trip to the hospital had given her a reprieve, but she could no longer delay the inevitable. She had to do what she dreaded most—cause Rafe even more pain.

He walked into the room just then, his dark eyes arrowing to hers. Her heart stumbled, a sudden clutch of yearning gripping her chest. She skimmed his freshly shaven jaw, the impossible breadth of his shoulders, the appealing contrast of his olive skin against the bright white fabric of his clean shirt. He was so handsome, so brave, so much like everything she'd ever wanted in a man.

But their time together was done.

"I filled the prescription," he said, his gravelly voice kicking off a jumble of nerves. "If you're ready, we can leave. I figured you'd stay with me."

She swallowed hard. There was no good way to say this, so she might as well blurt it out. "I'm going back to my hotel. I'll stay there until I decide what I'm going to do."

He went dead still. A sudden alertness entered his eyes. "And why is that?" he asked, his voice oddly neutral.

She forced herself to hold his gaze. "I'm not going to lie to you, Rafe. The past few days, the time in the barn… I can never thank you enough for that. You changed my life. You healed me." He'd given her back her sexuality, a debt she could never repay. "But now…"

"Now what?"

She inhaled around the pressure in her chest. "That rape changed me. I'm not the same person I used to be." Her cousin's treachery and those final moments with Ortiz had driven that home—bringing back the horrific feeling of helplessness, the shocking sense of betrayal, the terrifying vulnerability she never wanted to experience again.

Rafe crossed his arms. "Neither of us are. So what's your point?"

"It's that…something died in me that night. I just…I don't have it in me anymore to do this."

His jaw tensed, and her heart drummed hard. He was angry. She could see it in his rigid stance, the tension radiating from his frame. "And exactly what is it that we're doing?"

"Having a relationship." Taking a risk. She couldn't open herself up and trust someone that deeply.

Not even Rafe.

"So you're giving up. You're running again." Anger crept into his voice.

"No, I—"

"The hell you're not. You said you were trying to protect me back when your father died. I get that. But that's not what it's about this time. This time you're protecting yourself."

Unable to bear his scrutiny, she dropped her gaze to her lap and twisted her hands. "Maybe I am. I don't know. I just…don't feel the same." She felt hollow inside, empty, and he deserved far more.

"I'm sorry," she whispered, knowing the words were inadequate.

For several painful heartbeats, he held her gaze. Then he reached into his pocket, fished out the prescription he'd filled and tossed it her way. As she caught the plastic vial, he turned to go.

But then he glanced back. "Run if you have to, Gabi. Just don't expect me to be here waiting if you ever decide to stop."

He turned and walked away.

Two days later, Rafe was still trying to come to grips with Gabi's rejection as he sat in his father's apartment, watching him sleep. She'd ended their affair. She'd made her feelings clear. There was no point replaying her words, no point hoping she'd change her mind.

So why couldn't he accept it? Why did it feel so wrong?

He scrubbed his hand over his face and sighed. Because he was delusional, that was why. He was trying to convince himself that she loved him when she'd definitely broken things off.

It wasn't as if she'd caught him unprepared. Hell, he'd even felt the same way—that they'd changed. That too many years had gone by to resurrect the past.

But that was before he'd realized he still loved her.

He shook his head. Enough was enough. He had to accept the truth. No matter what they'd shared, no matter how deep his feelings for her, she didn't want him in her life. And no amount of wishful thinking could alter that fact.

His father stirred, drawing his gaze. At least one good thing had come from this fiasco. The king had pardoned his father as a reward to Rafe for saving his life.

His father opened his eyes. "Rafe?" he rasped.

"I'm here." His throat suddenly constricted, he scooted his chair closer to the bed. A once vibrant man, his father was wasting away—his hair gone from the chemotherapy, his skin loose from the weight he'd dropped, his body riddled with disease.

"I need to thank you...."

"What?" Rafe leaned nearer to hear.

His father cleared his throat. "I never thanked you... for getting me out of jail."

Rafe grimaced at that. "It was the least I could do. It was my fault you got arrested in the first place."

"No. You were right. I never should have tried to pull

off that heist." He leaned forward, racked by a deep, wrenching cough.

Rafe grabbed the cup of melting crushed ice from the bedside table and held it out, angling the straw. His father took a sip, then waved him off.

"I shouldn't have asked you to help," he continued, his voice stronger. "You'd changed, taken your life in another direction. And I should have respected that."

Rafe eased out his breath, the hard knot of guilt he'd harbored for years unfurling inside.

"You did the right thing, you know," his father added, turning his head on the pillow to meet his eyes. "This kind of lifestyle…it used to be different. But the world's changing. You need to do something better with your life."

"I do a pretty good business with the gem shop. At least it pays my bills."

"And you're going to be a knight." Fierce pride tinged his father's voice.

Rafe snorted at that. "Yeah." The king was determined to knight him, despite Rafe's efforts to turn the honor down. The king credited him with saving the royal family, a story the media continued to hype. They'd made him out to be some kind of hero, to both his parents' delight.

His father chuckled, the familiar sound warming Rafe's heart. How many years had it been since he'd heard him laugh? "A knight in the family," he mused. "Isn't that something?"

"It's pretty ironic, considering all the crimes we pulled off over the years. The aristocrats will have a stroke."

"Hell, they're no better than we are. Most of them are corrupt."

Rafe nodded, remembering the prime minister. "Some of them definitely are."

His father's expression sobered. For a minute he didn't speak. Then he reached out and touched Rafe's hand. "Listen, Rafe. I wasted a lot of years in jail because I didn't listen to you—years I could have spent with your mother and you boys. Now it's time you listen to me. Don't make my mistake. Don't let your ego steer you wrong. Life's too short." His face turning pale, he slumped back against the pillows and closed his eyes.

Alarmed, Rafe lunged forward. "Dad?"

But his father shook his head. "I'm just tired. I need to rest. Come back later, and we'll talk more."

Rafe squeezed his fragile hand. "I will. You need anything before I go? More water?"

"No, I'm fine."

Rafe waited, listening to his father's slow breathing, watching his face grow slack with sleep. And a painful contraction gripped his throat, the stark, brutal weight of reality settling in. His father would be gone soon. He didn't have much time left.

A fierce pressure forming behind his eyelids, Rafe rose and went into the hall. His mother emerged from the kitchen, wiping her hands on a towel. Her anxious eyes met his. "How is he?" A small woman, she'd added pounds and wrinkles over the years, but her face still held vestiges of the beauty she'd once been.

"He's asleep."

Her eyes searched his. "You'll come back for dinner?"

"Yeah. I'll be back. I need to stop at the store, take care of some bills." Try to get his life back on track.

"Your brothers will be here."

Rafe bent and gave his mother's soft cheek a kiss. "Good." They hadn't completely healed the rift between them, but they'd made a start.

But as he headed to the elevator, his father's words echoed in his mind. He'd claimed that his ego had misled him. He'd warned Rafe not to repeat his mistake.

But how was Rafe making a mistake? How was his ego leading him astray? His thoughts winged back to Gabi, and he frowned. Her rejection had stung his pride, no doubt about that. He loved her, but she obviously didn't feel the same.

Or did she?

Mulling that over, he punched the button for the elevator and waited for it to arrive. He thought back to that moment in the chapel, envisioning her ashen face, the numb, shocked look in her eyes as she'd held that gun. She'd been injured, bleeding. Traumatized.

The last time Ortiz had attacked her, she'd fled. And unless Rafe missed his guess, she was still running, still reacting the same way.

Was he?

That thought jarred him. The elevator arrived, and he stepped inside, then pressed the button for the bottom floor. But as the elevator started downward, the question kept hammering his mind, refusing to go away. He'd blamed their breakup on her. She was the one who'd called it off. But what if he was also to blame? What it instead of doing what he had to, giving her the space she thought she needed, he was letting his wounded ego and insecurities drive him away—just as he had before?

The elevator jolted to a stop. The doors slid open,

and he strode out, not wanting to believe he'd repeated his mistake. But he couldn't banish the doubts.

They'd faced plenty of obstacles to their relationship in the past, real impediments they'd had to overcome. But he'd come a long way from his childhood. He had an education now. He had money, thanks to the gem-dealing business he ran. Becoming a knight would eliminate their social gap, so even that didn't stand in their way.

And God knew he loved her. When he'd realized Ortiz had her cornered, he'd been scared out of his mind, frantic to make sure she'd survived.

The only thing standing in their way now was her lack of feelings for him.

He exited the apartment building, then stopped on the sidewalk and frowned at the cars zipping by. Gabi had claimed that the rape had changed her, that she was no longer capable of love. But was that true? Could she have trusted him to make love to her if she wasn't in love with him?

The truth barreled through him, and he closed his eyes. She loved him. He'd seen it in her eyes and in her efforts to shield him from harm. But she was stuck in the painful past, still battling the emotions of that rape. And instead of helping her through the trauma, instead of behaving like the hero the newspapers claimed he was and staying at her side, he'd let his pride dictate his behavior and walked away.

Disgusted, he headed to his car. He was a fool, all right. But like his father, he'd learned from his mistakes.

He and Gabi belonged together.

Now he had to convince her of that.

Chapter 15

Clouds hung low over the Ferrer estate, their steel bottoms clinging to the ancient watchtower, the cool wind heavy with the threat of rain. Gabi stood in her abandoned garden, watching the trees dip and sway before the gusting breeze, and waited for the storm to roll in.

She'd loved thunderstorms as a child. She'd loved feeling the excitement crackling the air, the exhilaration as nature unleashed its savage fury, the stark beauty of lightning sizzling against the sky.

But her life had changed since then. She'd lost everything she held dear. Her father had died. She'd lived through hell and survived. She'd had to give up Rafe.

The wind bore down, bringing a splattering of icy drops. Reluctant to return to the boarded-up house, she waded through the weeds to a small stone bench, then sat, her bandaged arm throbbing in its sling. Tugging her sweater closer around her, she watched a raptor riding the thermals in the somber sky—a bearded vulture, Reino Antiguo's symbol, like the one on that signet ring.

She wrinkled her brow, her thoughts returning to Ortiz. His death should have brought her closure. Instead, she felt lost and confused—about her life, her job, *Rafe*.

She heaved out a sigh, feeling as adrift as that soaring bird. Frankly, she had no idea what to do. With both Ortiz and the prime minister dead, she no longer had to hide. She had no need to run, no one threatening her. She could stay in País Vell, reopen her estate and resume her former life.

Or she could sell her father's corporation and leave. She had money, freedom, time. She could live abroad and reinvent herself. She had nothing to hold her here.

Except Rafe.

She flushed despite the cool wind, the guilt she'd ignored for days returning with a vengeance now. She'd hurt him. Terribly. While he'd repeatedly risked his life to save hers, acting with honor and courage, she'd panicked and pushed him away.

And why was that? She loved him. She couldn't deny that anymore. She loved his bravery, his honor, his deep-rooted sense of justice. And she knew that he loved her. He'd proven it every way he could—in his ravaging kiss, the tender way he'd made love, his attempts to protect her at every turn.

So why the panic? Why the desperate need to send him away? Why try so hard to convince herself that she didn't feel what she did?

The wind gusted again, blowing her hair loose, and she gathered it up, trying in vain to control it with just one hand. And then she stilled. *Control.* Was that her problem? Was she trying to stay in control?

Her eyes narrowed on the dancing trees. Growing up, she'd longed for excitement. Her father had meant well, but his attempts to protect her, along with the restrictions of her social class, had made her feel confined. Acting had provided an outlet, a way to break free from her stifling existence, even if it was only pretend.

And then she'd met Rafe.

He'd been the ideal man for her—sexy, potent, taboo. He came from an off-limits world. He'd broken all of society's rules, yet still had an honorable core. And he'd indulged her need for adventure—teaching her how to scale walls, pick locks and creep through the dead of night—while keeping her perfectly safe.

But that rape had shattered her security, destroying her confidence in authority, changing everything she'd believed about the world. She'd felt defenseless, exposed, unable to trust anyone. Completely out of control.

Seeing Ortiz again had brought the terror back. When he'd trapped her in that hallway, she'd relived her worst nightmare, experiencing the vulnerability she hated most.

She'd killed Ortiz, but the attack had left her spooked. So she'd lashed out at the man she loved.

And let the police chief win.

She closed her eyes, hating this view of herself, but she couldn't deny the truth. She'd healed sexually in the past few days. She'd even stood up to Ortiz. But she was still cowering emotionally, still afraid to expose herself to hurt.

And until she confronted that final fear, she'd stay stuck in the vicious past.

She hesitated, knowing she was at a crossroads, that this was the moment of truth. She either had to take a chance, take the final, emotional step and entrust her heart to Rafe, or say goodbye forever to love.

She made a face. What was she thinking? Rafe would never hurt her. He was the most loyal man she knew! But he was right; she couldn't expect him to wait forever. She had to hurry and find him, then beg him for another chance—if it wasn't already too late.

She leaped to her feet and rushed across the garden toward the house, ignoring the pain in her throbbing arm. But a man appeared on the overgrown walkway, blocking her way.

Rafe.

Wondering if she'd somehow conjured him up, she came to a halt. But he was real. She took in his short, windblown hair, those mesmerizing black eyes, his strong, wide shoulders that could carry her burdens for years. Her heart swelled with love. A lump lodged in her throat, the emotions she'd bottled for years threatening to break free.

"The door was open," he said. "I hope you don't mind that I came in."

She shook her head. She tried to speak, but her mouth wobbled badly, and she bit down hard on her lip. "I was just going to find you," she managed to say.

He stalked steadily toward her. Her heart began to thud. "And why was that?" he asked, his gaze locked on hers.

A maelstrom swirled inside her, fierce needs tumbling and clamoring to get loose. "Because I love you."

He stopped dead in his tracks. "What?"

"I love you. I never stopped. Oh, Rafe, I'm so sorry. I was such a coward. I was afraid and I pushed you away."

He quickly closed the distance between them. He cupped her face with his work-worn hands, his expression filled with so much tenderness that hot tears misted her eyes.

"I'm the one who's sorry," he said, his voice hoarse. "I never should have left you. Can you forgive me for that?"

She tried to smile through her tears, but failed. "There's nothing to forgive."

He searched her eyes, as if to convince himself of the truth. Then he lowered his mouth to hers and swept her into a kiss—soft and reverent and sure. She responded with a sigh, giving herself over to the pleasure, the warmth, the absolute rightness of being in his arms. Rafe was the one man she could depend on, the man who excited her, challenged her, complementing her in every way.

Long moments later, he broke the kiss, then rested his forehead against hers. "I love you, Gabi. I made a mistake and let you go, but I won't do that again." He drew back slightly, his eyes suddenly uncertain. "You'll marry me, won't you?"

More tears leaked from her eyes. "Yes," she whispered, her heart expanding. "I'll marry you."

He kissed her again. Then he enfolded her in his arms, taking care not to bump her sling. She rested her cheek against his chest, absorbing the strong, steady beat of his heart.

"You know," she said with a smile. "This is the second time you've proposed to me here."

"I remember."

She pulled back slightly and shot him a teasing glance. "I'm still waiting for the ring."

"I finally found the right one." He leaned back, reached into his pocket, and drew out a small velvet box bearing his gem dealership's name—Navarro, S.A.

Her heart changed its beat. A sudden swarm of nerves erupted inside her, and she dropped her gaze to the box. He flipped open the top.

An enormous chameleon diamond winked back, shimmering in shades of silvery blues and greens. "Oh, Rafe," she whispered, picking it up. "It's amazing. I've never seen anything like it."

"I thought of you the minute I saw it. It's just like you are—beautiful, fascinating, always changing…."

His strong hand traced her jaw. His serious black eyes met hers. "Be sure about this, Gabi. Because once that ring's on your finger, you're mine forever. I'm not going to let you go."

She slid on the ring. And then she pulled his head down to hers and kissed him, sheer happiness bursting inside.

But then he pulled away. "About my business… I can sell it if you want. I'll move wherever you need to go."

Her heart rolled. "You'd do that for me? Forfeit the business you've built?"

"I'll do anything for you. Don't you know that by now?"

Her throat closed up. She blinked back another onslaught of tears. She did know that. She always had. It was why she loved him so much.

"I'd like to stay in País Vell," she said. She glanced at the neglected garden, the medieval fortress she'd loved as a child, and an intense feeling of *rightness* lodged inside. "I'm done running. I have roots here, the same as you do. I think we should open up the estate, and fill it with laughter and sunshine. Children, too."

His wicked smile made her blood heat. "I think I can accommodate that."

"But about our jobs…"

"I'm serious, Gabi. I can go wherever you want. Or you can sell your company. My gem business can support us both."

Still holding him close, she considered that. "I always thought I'd sell my father's business once I took down Ortiz. But now…" A thought swirled through her, an idea that had lurked in the back of her mind for months. "There's something I've been thinking about, ever since I found out what my father was doing."

"Spying?"

She nodded. "You told me once that you liked the adrenaline rush, the danger of being a thief."

His mouth twisted. "These last few days might have cured me of that."

"I don't think so. That's one of the things we always had in common, that we both like adventure."

"So?"

"So it just occurred to me…our companies are the perfect front."

"Front for what? Don't tell me you want to take up a life of crime?"

"No, not crime. I definitely want to work for the good guys. But we could start moonlighting." Excitement surged inside her. "Think about it, Rafe. The king still needs to root out traitors. And other people could use our help, too. So we could start a secret sideline."

"Being thieves?"

"*Good* thieves. And we'd be discreet, only operating by word of mouth. It's perfect for us, Rafe. I've got the connections. You've got the skills, and you know people we can hire if we can't do a job ourselves. People like… like Miguel, who helped us break into Ortiz's hard drive. And with your gem business and my communications company we'd have access everywhere, in all sorts of circles, all over the world. And you have to admit we make a good team."

He shook his head, but a gleam entered his eyes, and she could tell he was already hooked.

"So what do you say?" she asked.

Thunder rumbled around them. He swept her into his arms, flashing her a hot, carnal grin that brought a rush of lust to her blood. "I say we take the dust cover off one of those beds inside and negotiate that."

He strode with her from the garden, and she held tight to the man she loved. They'd traveled a rocky path. They'd suffered loneliness and tragedy and loss along the way. But they were stronger now. They'd defeated their enemies and battled their way back to each other's arms.

And could finally seize the happiness they deserved.

* * * * *

SUSPENSE

Heartstopping stories of intrigue and mystery—
where true love always triumphs.

COMING NEXT MONTH
AVAILABLE NOVEMBER 22, 2011

#1683 A CAVANAUGH CHRISTMAS
Cavanaugh Justice
Marie Ferrarella

#1684 CAPTAIN'S CALL OF DUTY
The Kelley Legacy
Cindy Dees

#1685 COPPER LAKE SECRETS
Marilyn Pappano

#1686 MILLIONAIRE'S LAST STAND
Small-Town Scandals
Elle Kennedy

REQUEST YOUR FREE BOOKS!
2 FREE NOVELS PLUS 2 FREE GIFTS!

ROMANTIC

SUSPENSE

Sparked by Danger, Fueled by Passion.

YES! Please send me 2 FREE Harlequin® Romantic Suspense novels and my 2 FREE gifts (gifts are worth about $10). After receiving them, if I don't wish to receive any more books, I can return the shipping statement marked "cancel." If I don't cancel, I will receive 4 brand-new novels every month and be billed just $4.49 per book in the U.S. or $5.24 per book in Canada. That's a saving of at least 14% off the cover price! It's quite a bargain! Shipping and handling is just 50¢ per book in the U.S. and 75¢ per book in Canada.* I understand that accepting the 2 free books and gifts places me under no obligation to buy anything. I can always return a shipment and cancel at any time. Even if I never buy another book, the two free books and gifts are mine to keep forever.

240/340 HDN FEFR

Name   (PLEASE PRINT)

Address   Apt. #

City   State/Prov.   Zip/Postal Code

Signature (if under 18, a parent or guardian must sign)

Mail to the **Reader Service:**
IN U.S.A.: P.O. Box 1867, Buffalo, NY 14240-1867
IN CANADA: P.O. Box 609, Fort Erie, Ontario L2A 5X3

Not valid for current subscribers to Harlequin Romantic Suspense books.

Want to try two free books from another line?
Call 1-800-873-8635 or visit www.ReaderService.com.

* Terms and prices subject to change without notice. Prices do not include applicable taxes. Sales tax applicable in N.Y. Canadian residents will be charged applicable taxes. Offer not valid in Quebec. This offer is limited to one order per household. All orders subject to credit approval. Credit or debit balances in a customer's account(s) may be offset by any other outstanding balance owed by or to the customer. Please allow 4 to 6 weeks for delivery. Offer available while quantities last.

Your Privacy—The Reader Service is committed to protecting your privacy. Our Privacy Policy is available online at www.ReaderService.com or upon request from the Reader Service.

We make a portion of our mailing list available to reputable third parties that offer products we believe may interest you. If you prefer that we not exchange your name with third parties, or if you wish to clarify or modify your communication preferences, please visit us at www.ReaderService.com/consumerschoice or write to us at Reader Service Preference Service, P.O. Box 9062, Buffalo, NY 14269. Include your complete name and address.

HRS11B

*Lucy Flemming and Ross Mitchell shared a magical,
sexy Christmas weekend together six years ago.
This Christmas, history may repeat itself when they find
themselves stranded in a major snowstorm...
and alone at last.*

Read on for a sneak peek from
IT HAPPENED ONE CHRISTMAS
by Leslie Kelly.

Available December 2011, only from Harlequin® Blaze™.

EYEING THE GRAY, THICK SKY through the expansive wall of windows, Lucy began to pack up her photography gear. The Christmas party was winding down, only a dozen or so people remaining on this floor, which had been transformed from cubicles and meeting rooms to a holiday funland. She smiled at those nearest to her, then, seeing the glances at her silly elf hat, she reached up to tug it off her head.

Before she could do it, however, she heard a voice. A deep, male voice—smooth and sexy, and so not Santa's.

"I appreciate you filling in on such short notice. I've heard you do a terrific job."

Lucy didn't turn around, letting her brain process what she was hearing. Her whole body had stiffened, the hairs on the back of her neck standing up, her skin tightening into tiny goose bumps. Because that voice sounded so familiar. *Impossibly* familiar.

It can't be.

"It sounds like the kids had a great time."

Unable to stop herself, Lucy began to turn around, wondering if her ears—and all her other senses—were deceiving her. After all, six years was a long time, the mind could play tricks. What were the odds that she'd bump into *him,* here? And today of all days. December 23.

Six years exactly. Was that really possible?

One look—and the accompanying frantic thudding of her heart—and she knew her ears and brain were working just fine. Because it was *him.*

"Oh, my God," he whispered, shocked, frozen, staring as thoroughly as she was. "Lucy?"

She nodded slowly, not taking her eyes off him, wondering why the years had made him even more attractive than ever. It didn't seem fair. Not when she'd spent the past six years thinking he must have started losing that thick, golden-brown hair, or added a spare tire to that trim, muscular form.

No.

The man was gorgeous. Truly, without-a-doubt, mouthwateringly handsome, every bit as hot as he'd been the first time she'd laid eyes on him. She'd been twenty-two, he one year older.

They'd shared an amazing holiday season.

And had never seen one another again.

Until now.

Find out what happens in
IT HAPPENED ONE CHRISTMAS
by Leslie Kelly.
Available December 2011, only from Harlequin® Blaze™

HBEXP1211

ROMANTIC
SUSPENSE

USA TODAY BESTSELLING AUTHOR

MARIE FERRARELLA

Brings you another exciting installment from

CAVANAUGH
JUSTICE

A Cavanaugh Christmas

When Detective Kaitlyn Two Feathers follows a kidnapping case outside her jurisdiction, she enlists the aid of Detective Thomas Cavelli. Still reeling from the discovery that his father was a Cavanaugh, Thomas takes the case, thinking it will be a nice distraction…until Kaitlyn becomes his ultimate distraction. As the case heats up and time is running out, Thomas must prove to Kaitlyn that he is trustworthy and risk it all for the one thing they both never thought they'd find—love.

Available November 22 wherever books are sold!

www.Harlequin.com

HRS27753